GABRIEL'S TREASURE

WHEELS & HOGS GARAGE
BOOK 3

D.M. EARL

Copyright @ 2015 D. M. Earl
Published by D. M. Earl

All rights reserved. Except for use in any review, the reproduction or utilization of this work in whole or in any part in any form by any electronic, mechanical or any other means, now or hereafter invented including photocopying, recording, information storage and retrieval systems-except in the case of brief quotations embodied in the critical article or reviews-without permission in writing from the author. This book may not be resold or redistributed without the express consent of the author.

For any questions or comments please email the author directly at DM@DMEARL.COM

This book is a work of fiction. All characters, events and places portrayed in this book are products of the author's imagination and are either fictitious or are used fictitiously. Any similarity to real persons, living or deceased is purely coincidental and not intentional.

This book contains sexual encounters, consensual and graphic language that some readers may find objectionable. It contains graphic material that is not suitable for anyone under the age of 18.

Romantic Erotic Mature Audience.

ACKNOWLEDGMENTS

There are so many people that have a part in this book. Without each and every one of you Gabriel's story would never have come to life.

To my Betas who no matter what always make time for me and my books. Their dedication and love of reading has guided me to the best possible story and also assisted me in making this the best Book 3 it could be. Without these ladies this project would never be completed.

My PA **Laura Barcenas** who has been a life saver. Thanks, Laura, for always being so positive and full of life. With you having my back and handling a lot of the social media has given me more time to do what I do best... write.

To two women who have had my back it seems like forever. Always pimping, sharing and getting my name out there. A huge shout-out to **Pam Buchanan** and **Nancy Huddleston**. I am honored that ya'll have been there for me and have gotten my name out there in the social media arena.

To all the Bloggers who have helped me over the last year with each and every one of my releases. I can never repay you for all of your support and I hope you realize how much I value each and every one of you.

Love between the Sheets and **Silla Webb @ Momma's Secret Book Obsession** a huge shout-out for your help in my release blitz, blog tour and the release party. You both are so professional and take so much off my shoulders. I appreciate you both so very much.

Margreet Asselbergs- You are my ROCK. In all this time you have never told me no. Even when you were working on your own stuff you always have my back. For that I am forever in your debt. I admire your professionalism, dedication and am honored to call you not only my illustrator, formatter, designer but also my friend.

Karen Hrdlicka- I so appreciate you taking the time to give Gabriel's Treasure a critical edit to make sure everything worked and was in order. Your critical eye makes each of my books as close to perfect as they can be.

Tee Tate-Thank you for taking on a newbie and giving me some great pointers and tips regarding writing. I appreciate your time and effort on this book. Your editing skills have made it a better book. I plan on using your tips on all future WIP.

Katie- a huge thank you for squeezing in this book for the last look and proofreading on a very tight time line Your eye for great detail made the final run through that much better. I am lucky to have found you. Appreciate your quick turn-around.

Dana Hook- thank you for opening my eyes to how my way might not always be the only way. Your dedication to your skill and the heart you put into each piece of work you touch is amazing. I know in my heart you always have my back even when we are bumping heads.

To my cousin **Tina**, whose expertise in the nursing field guided me through the different processes when dealing with cancer. She took the time to provide me with all aspects of how treatment can and will affect a person. She also was always there to answer my questions. 'Cuz I love you and sincerely thank you for your help. Your insight and knowledge made this book true to life.

To each and every **Reade**r who has purchased one of my books, took the time to read, comment, review and let me know how much they enjoyed the story. Because of you I am able to live my dream. Thank you.

Finally the one person who means the world to me. **Chuck**-Baby, I would have never gotten this far without your support and love. There are no words to express how much you mean to me. Thanks for being a part of my dream. Love ya, baby.

CHAPTER ONE

PRESENT

(Gabriel)

The panic hits me immediately in the center of my chest as my breathing quickens. Feeling the sweat run down my neck, I feel the shaking begin in my hands. The cravings have hit me again and I have no control over it. These feelings are so intense I stand quickly, releasing Fern's hand as I bend down to whisper in her ear, "Be back in a minute, sugar." She nods in understanding as I turn, rushing out of the room with no idea where I'm heading. I just know I need some time away from the crowded room of people.

Briskly walking from my wife's room in this godforsaken hospital the door closes behind me. I'm not sure which one of them came to check on me, but I really don't have it in me to hide these feelings right now. I pick up my pace. Halfway down the hallway, Des calls from behind me, "Doc, hold up."

Knowing he will follow me no matter what, I stop

and put my shoulder to the corridor wall, waiting for him to catch up.

When he's beside me his hand goes to my shoulder, squeezing tightly. Instead of feeling closed in, I'm comforted. Des puts some pressure into his squeeze, which grabs my attention. I glance his way seeing not only concern but also the troubled look in his eyes.

Directing me to the small lounge for family members, he pushes me down into a chair while asking, "Doc, want some coffee?"

I think of the nickname with disgust. Even with my background as a medic in the service, there's nothing I can do for my wife.

Nodding my head I reply, "Sure. Thanks, Des."

He comes back with two cups of coffee, taking a seat across from me, handing me mine.

"Okay, talk to me, Doc. What the fuck's going on? After listening to Trinity, I thought you would be feeling optimistic regarding Fern's condition."

I still remain silent, because I know if I open my mouth all my fears and worries will come barreling out. Fuck, I run my hands through my hair trying to get my shit together. God, I could use one of those damn energy drinks or pills I have been taking. I feel so drained and tired. Des comes across and sits next to me. I turn to see what he's doing, and the next thing I know he is grasping my shoulders and pulling me in for a man hug, which, until this very moment, I didn't realize how much I needed.

As soon as my head hits his shoulder, I feel the

pressure in my eyes and fight to hold it in when he tells me harshly, "Dude, pull your shit together. Fuck it, take a minute or two but, Doc, you don't want Fern to see you like this. That woman of yours has enough going on besides worrying about your sorry ass."

Leave it to Des to get right to the point. Trying to catch the sob as it escapes, I feel the wetness running down my cheeks. I don't know how long this goes on before I pull away. Des stands up and walks across to the desk, where the attendant sits playing on her phone. Watching him approach her, I reach in my pocket and grab one of the pills, swallowing it down with my lukewarm coffee. When she looks up and sees Des, her eyes widen as he asks her for some tissues. She reaches under the desk and gives him the box and, without even looking at her, he comes back with the tissues, placing them on my lap. Grabbing a couple I wipe my face and blow my nose, feeling like such a pussy. Never have I cried in front of anyone but Fern. Not because I am a macho asshole. There just has never been anything worth crying about. I have always believed that we are in charge of our own destiny. But not knowing the outcome of all of this has my emotions all over the place.

"Doc, I don't have a fucking clue what you're going through or feeling so I'm not gonna act like I do. What I do know is, with this new development, we have to keep the faith. No matter what happens, you have to be positive, especially in front of Fern. So do whatever you have to do to pull your shit together, my friend, because we need to get back to her. I'm sure she's trying to get out of that bed, and I'm not sure how long Dee Dee can keep her from doing just that."

Looking my friend in the eyes, I pull myself together and we head back to the room Fern is in.

CHAPTER TWO

PRESENT

(Fern)

Watching my husband and Des leave, the feeling in the room changes. For a split second, after Trinity shared her secret with all of us, I felt some renewed faith and hope that maybe there is a chance I could beat this awful disease. But watching Gabriel almost lose it before he exited, something deep inside me felt his pain. My poor Gabriel has been through hell and back with all that has happened to me. Why he is still with me, I have no idea

Dee Dee approaches my bedside. "Fern, he will be just fine, probably needing some air to take in all this information. How you holding up?"

"I'm trying to stay positive, but just knowing this is my last effort scares the crap out of me. What happens if it doesn't work? Where does that leave me?"

"You heard what the doctor told you, Fern, you have to stay positive and keep fighting. They wouldn't be going through with the transplant if they didn't think it would work."

Nodding her way, I sit up in my hospital bed gazing at all of my "family," or as Des calls it, the Horde, my weary body starts to fail me. Exhausted beyond my limits, I try to stay focused on what everyone is saying, even though it is coming across mumbled and unclear. I know my pain pump just released a dose of morphine because I am getting that foggy feeling. After a couple of minutes go by, I give Dee Dee a look. As I try to get more comfortable, Dee Dee's sharp eyes take me in. After watching and observing me for a minute she looks around the room, telling everyone it's time to go and let me rest. I nod in her direction as the drugs start to work, knowing I will be asleep in no time at all.

One by one they come to me and give me a kiss or a hand squeeze. I try to stay focused, but when it's Daisy's turn, she looks pale with dark circles under her eyes.

"You doing okay, sweetie?" Her eyes shoot up to meet mine and before she can hide it, I see the pain in her eyes. "Daisy, what's going on? Talk to me please. You're worrying me."

Her eyes shift to see if anyone is listening, especially her mom, Dee Dee.

"Nothing is wrong, Fern. Everything is great." She tries to make her tone sound happy but doesn't come close to succeeding.

"Kiddo, look at me. No matter what I am going through, I'm always here for you, sweetie. Okay?"

She nods, leaning in, giving me a soft kiss, then turns, walking out of the room looking like she has the weight of the world on her shoulders.

By the time Cadence gets to me, I am fighting to keep my eyes open. He leans down, whispering in my ear, "No matter what, I'm not lettin' ya go, Fern. Don't stop fighting, 'cause Hope needs you in her life just like Trinity and I do."

Kissing my forehead, he gently caresses my cheek, moving aside for Trinity to give me a peck also. As she leans toward me, I feel intense warmth in my body suddenly, and struggling with opening my eyes I see little Hope staring at me intently. This has to be the drugs playing with me because, I swear, she just smiled at me. As Trinity turns to Cadence and they head out of the room, they take that warmth with them.

Suddenly I feel chilled. Dee Dee sees me trembling and grabs another blanket, placing it over me. Sitting on the edge of my bed, she holds my hand softly as she speaks to me.

"Go ahead and sleep, my friend. I will watch over you until Gabriel and Des return. Sweet dreams."

Squeezing her hand, I glance her way and put to words what is weighing on my mind.

"Worried about Daisy, Dee Dee. Something is up with her. Can't put my finger on it, but you need to keep an eye on her. Is she having problems in school? She isn't herself and you know how mean kids can be, Dee Dee."

"I noticed some subtle things too, Fern. Spoke to

Des about it, but with everything going on I haven't had the time to sit her down and speak to her. I will rectify that as soon as I can. She's distant and seems to want to be by herself more lately. She isn't active in her usual activities either, now that I think of it. This will be addressed, Fern, promise. Now, back to you. How you doing?"

"Dee Dee, I am so scared. I don't want to die but I can feel my body giving up. Trying to hang on and after what Trinity just..."

I take a moment to catch my breath. Dee Dee brings a cup of water with a straw to my lips and graciously I take a couple of sips to moisten my mouth.

"I am so grateful to Trinity for all she has put together. Believe me, praying it works, but if Hope and I don't match that is my last hope."

Looking at her I kind of giggle, "No pun intended" as she smiles at me. Dee Dee clears her throat and gives it to me direct, as she always does.

"Fern, you can't lose faith. This is a miracle in itself with Trinity having the baby and thinking to look into an umbilical cord stem cell transplant. I have a good feeling on this and totally believe in the power of prayer. We will start the prayer circle and I know God will hear us, as you have been through enough. But it is all on your shoulders, my friend, you must continue to fight and this is the biggest fight of your life. Honey, you have to want to live, that's the only way you will get through this and live. Now can you do that for me, Fern, can you fight like you never have before? We will all support you, but you got to do this for yourself because that's the only way you will get through this."

Yawning as I pull the covers up to my neck, thinking on her words, I glance at my longtime friend, squeezing her hand with what little strength I have left.

"Dee Dee, I swear to you on everything I hold precious that I will battle this with everything I have left. But I need you to promise me that if this doesn't work, or it fails, and I lose this battle, please watch out for my Gabriel. He'll need all of you to support him because I don't think he will be able to handle it."

As tears start to slowly run down her cheeks, she reaches over, squeezing my shoulder.

"That isn't going to happen, so no need for me to promise that. We always have each other's back, sweetie, you know that."

Knowing she is trying to put me off, I actually feel a bit upset as I again request.

"Dee, that aside, I need that promise. Without me, Gabriel only has the Horde and I need to know in my heart that if something does happen you will watch out for him, support him, and eventually help him to move on and continue living. Knowing him, he will lock down and let his life pass him by and I don't want that. So here and now, please give me your word that you will make sure he truly lives and not only exists. He deserves to have love and have a family in his life, if it is with me or someone else eventually."

She slowly turns away from me for a minute, trying to compose herself and softly replies to my request.

"Fern, the last thing I want to think about is you not being here and Gabriel moving on, but if that is what you want, then I will promise you that if the unthinkable happens, I will honor your wishes and support Gabriel in his time of need. Okay?"

I just nod my head.

Dee Dee can see that I am fighting the effect of the medicine and starts running her hands through my hair gently.

"Sweet Fern, go ahead and sleep my friend. I am here for you always and will watch over you until both Gabriel and Des return."

As I fall into a drug-induced sleep, my mind takes me back to Gabriel's and my first encounter.

CHAPTER THREE

PAST ~FRESHMAN MEETING~

(Fern)

Walking through the corridor between classes at East High School with my head down, books held close to my chest, I feel the pressure building as an anxiety attack starts. Why does this always happen to me? No matter how hard I try to keep it together, these attacks keep happening. As all the other kids in my high school go about their day without a care in the world, I struggle to get from class to class.

Being quiet and shy has not helped me make a lot of friends. I knew being a freshman would be a hard transition. I just didn't realize how difficult that adjustment would be. As I continue to my least favorite class, English, I suddenly find myself flying forward as someone pushes me hard from behind. Losing my balance, I start to go down when I feel an arm grab me and pull me against what feels like a brick wall. Well, not exactly a wall, but a chest that feels like one. I hear something close to a growl, and as I take in a deep breath my heart starts to race. The cologne is familiar, all male and musky, and smells fresh like the great outdoors. I know immediately who has hold of me. He's in a couple of my classes and I am so totally in love with him.

Gabriel Murphy. Oh my God, he is holding me close and I can't breathe. Suddenly my entire body tingles and my lungs gasp for air. As I try to get some control over myself, I hear his deep-throated voice.

"Hey, asshole, what the hell was that? Why'd you push Fern?" He takes in a deep breath. "Sorry, for the language, Fern. He just really pissed me off. Shit, damn it, I mean sorry again. Guess you can see I cuss a lot."

I can hear the humor behind his words and just shake my head because any words that would come out are stuck in my throat. Struggling to reply, I feel his chest start to shake and I realize he is actually laughing.

"What's so funny? Why are you laughing?" I ask him. He looks intently at me with those intense emerald eyes.

"You're cute when you are flustered, you know that, right? I can't help it. I can feel your body giving off so many different emotions. I'm surprised you're even able to breathe, let alone stand. Take it easy, lil' Fern. I got you."

At his words my body seems to get warm and excited. My belly starts to feel funny as goose bumps appear on my arms. As gently as possible, Gabriel sets me back on my own two feet but keeps a grip on me so I don't lose my balance. Once I have my bearings, his arms fall to his sides and he watches me struggling. Finally, I glance his way.

"Who pushed me and why do you care, Gabriel? Was that supposed to be funny, because it definitely wasn't? I could have gotten hurt."

Gabriel puts both hands on my shoulders, holding me an arm's length away as his eyes take in my face then wander down my neck, stopping for a bit as he admires my budding breasts. Then his eyes linger on my belly before traveling down, watching my reaction the entire time. I feel my breath quicken as my nipples harden while my body suddenly wants to be close to his. The feeling intensifies when our eyes meet. His low, gravelly voice flows over me slowly, almost like what a caress would feel like I think to myself.

"Calm down. Don't get your feathers in a ruffle. It was Johnny Blackstone and my boys are taking care of him. Are you okay? Fern, take a deep breath, sugar. I'm only trying to help. You didn't get hurt, did you?" His hand gently cups my jaw and I lean into it without thinking.

My body still on fire from his perusal, I feel the blush covering my face and neck. His emerald eyes seem to get even greener as he smiles. Darn, he knows that I am crushing on him and it amuses him.

Just as I am ready to turn around and head to my class, he grabs my books and gently puts a hand on my back. "Let's get you to your next class, lil' Fern."

I don't like being called lil' Fern. I'm not a kid and think Gabriel should know that.

"Quit fucking calling me lil' Fern. I am not a child, Gabriel. Dammit, we are the same age you know."

Taken aback at the harsh words, he looks down at me.

"I wasn't treating you like a child. It's just that you're so tiny compared to me. That's all. Never noticed that before. In fact, missed a lot about you, Fern."

Hearing his words, I glance at him hesitantly. He looks at me so sincerely and I realize that my anger got the best of me again. I hesitantly smile his way, unsure on how to handle this situation. Gabriel seems so genuine but I am struggling with my anger and also with my crush on him.

Getting my emotions under control finally, I start to feel foolish and immature after all he did, saving me from falling down. I'm making a fool of myself.

"I'm sorry, Gabriel, I didn't mean to be such a baby. This just has flustered me. Thank you so much for helping me. I really appreciate it. I'm fine. Go ahead. I can make it to my next class. It is right around the corner."

As I try to pull away, he tightens his hold on me. Pulling me closer, his eyes look directly into mine for a minute. Gazing at me watching him, he slowly smiles a sexy as hell smile at me.

"I'm walking you to class, Fern, before we are both late. Let's go."

For some reason his being bossy actually makes me feel good. For the first time in a long time, I feel like someone actually cares about what happens to me. In the back of my head I thank Johnny Blackstone for the push.

When English class ends, I pick up my belongings and head to the door so I can make it back to my locker and change out books.

As I turn left down the corridor, I hear my name. Once again, I feel the warmth throughout my body as I see Gabriel. He's holding Johnny with both of his hands on Johnny's neck and pushing him toward me. As I watch, so does everyone in the hall. The hallway is crowded with onlookers. Once Johnny is directly in front of me, Gabriel half growls, half whispers, "Say it."

Johnny puts his head down, not meeting my eyes.

"Sorry, Fern. I didn't mean to push you."

Everyone waits for my reply, but I am frozen, staring into those green eyes that are watching me intently. "Don't feel sorry for him, Fern. He brought this on himself." How does he know what I am thinking?

"Johnny, I accept your apology but why did you push me?"

He grumbles until Gabriel tightens his grip.

"Just horsing around. Fern, you always have your head down or in your books. We thought it would be funny to watch you trying to hang on to your books and not fall."

At this Gabriel releases him, turning Johnny to face

him. The look on his face scares me and obviously Johnny too because he pees his jeans. Gabriel shoves him and Johnny goes down hard to his butt.

"Funny huh, Johnny?" Gabriel asks him while the crowd laughs. Johnny tries to hide his embarrassment. Feeling sorry for him, I grab the hoodie Gabriel holds and give it to Johnny. "Use this to cover up your...umm, well your wet pants."

As everyone turns and goes about their business, Gabriel grabs me by the elbow and guides me to my locker, not saying a word. He waits for me to change out my books and walks me to my next class. This is how it started, back in freshman year when Gabriel claimed me first as a friend, and then, later as his girlfriend.

CHAPTER FOUR

PRESENT ~ WATCHING ~

(Gabriel)

Dee Dee wiping her cheeks dry is the first thing I notice as I walk into the room. Des and I rush toward her as she moves off Fern's bed. She turns and goes immediately to Des as he pulls her close into his arms, holding tightly around her. I watch impatiently as Dee tries to pull herself together. Not sure what happened in our absence, my worried glance takes in Fern. She is sleeping with the covers up to her chin. Her fragile body looks so small and she has black circles under her eyes. My heart breaks just looking at what this disease is doing to my wife.

Des clears his throat and gives me a head nod. As I walk toward them, Dee Dee reaches out and takes my hand. Just the feel of her soft hand in mine brings back so many memories and emotional times when Fern would grab my hand for one reason or another. Trying to stay focused, I wait until Dee Dee seems able to explain what we walked into. She directs us to the farthest point in the room, away from Fern.

"Doc, she is really struggling. Even though this idea of Trinity's is great news, Fern is starting to shut down and prepare for the worst." Des shakes his head at Dee Dee and she continues, "Fern made me promise to watch over you in case she..."

Looking at the two people who are closer to Fern and me than our own families, seeing my reaction to her words must have clued them in that what they just told me is a deal breaker for me. Since she was diagnosed with cancer, Fern and I made a pact to always remain positive and have faith. Hearing the promise she extracted from Dee makes me think that her faith is wavering.

Giving both of them a hug, they remind me that if I need anything, they are a phone call away. I thank them and once they are gone, I turn down the lights, pull the recliner closer to Fern's bedside, and remove my flannel, jeans, belt, and shoes. I empty my pockets on the counter and pull my sleep pants, the pillow and blanket out of the closet. This has become my nightly routine. I refuse to leave Fern alone at night so the hospital obliges me and even found this recliner so I can sleep in her room night after night.

So after I am situated for the night, I put my hands behind my head, trying to relax, as my body hungers for the relief from the pills that give me a temporary reprieve. I don't want to have to take them but the need for them is increasing each day.

Looking at the woman in the hospital bed, knowing how I am letting her down kills me. This growing addiction to pills and energy drinks makes my guilt at keeping this secret from her eat at me. I glance at Fern who was petite to begin with, but now she is frail. Her hair has grown back from the last chemo treatments and is just above her shoulders. Her skin is transparent and she has dark circles under her sunken eyes. As I take everything in, I can't stop the ache in my heart. I see the truth, even though my heart and soul refuse to accept it. Looking up and down her body and listening to her breathing, watching the machines, it finally hits me hard. After all of this time, never once did I accept the fact I could very well lose all that is precious in my life. I have called Fern from the beginning *my treasure*.

Suddenly it is too much for me to bear and a sob escapes my lips. Sitting up in the recliner, trying to get my emotions under control, my body trembles from the force of accepting what is right in front of me. My eyes blur as tears leak out of them freely, running down my face as my heart rate increases. Feeling the panic and anxiety start, my body is instantly covered in sweat and my hands are shaking. Reaching in my pocket, I pop two pills into my mouth, chasing them with a huge gulp of the energy drink on the table. I won't make it if I lose her. Nothing else in this world means anything to me like Fern. She is the air I breathe and the sun that warms my body. She is what I call my home. Without her, I am just a shell with nothing and no purpose. Feeling the effects of the drink on my body, I try to control my mind as I am struggling to hold it together. As I lean forward, my hands on the bed, I rock back and forth with the knowledge that if the cord blood doesn't match with Fern, we are out of options.

Shoulders shaking, tears running freely, I don't hear the door opening but I feel a hand on my shoulder. Glancing around, I see Cadence as he moves in front and pulls me into his chest. I let it all go and thank God he takes it all without saying a word. For what seems like forever my body lets loose, all the emotions I have held on to for the last couple of years. I feel jumpy and edgy because the mixture I took has kicked in. Finally, as I try to pull myself together, Cad pulls a chair close and sits next to me, hanging on to my hand. Grabbing some tissues from the bedside table, I wipe my face then turn to look at him. His eyes are shining and I can see the agony behind them. He has been the one who has been there from the beginning of Fern's illness. When I couldn't be there, he helped with treatments, bedpans, cleaning vomit after chemo, and everything and anything in between. Never once has Cadence balked at helping Fern out. In fact, there were times when she would have to push him to leave because if he had his way, he would have moved in with us.

For Fern and me, being we couldn't have our own children, when Cadence came into our lives, he became the child we never had. He arrived into the Horde when he was in a terrible way, beaten half to death, and has turned into a man we are proud of. His love for Fern matches mine, just in a different way. I know he is suffering and as we turn to the woman who holds our hearts in her hands, we hang on to each other, praying that Trinity's efforts pay off.

As the night goes by, Cadence and I talk about nothing in particular, but having him here makes it just a bit easier. He leaves around midnight, coming back with some takeout food and a strawberry shake for Fern when she wakes up. We both move to the little table in the corner and start eating.

"So did the charity ride raise enough to save the house?" he asks.

Mouth full of burger, I nod my head, chasing down my food with a sip of my vanilla shake. "Yeah, we are overwhelmed with the amount of money that was raised. For the first time since Fern was diagnosed with cancer, we are current on our house payment and all other bills. We have been talking about remodeling some of the house because it is old and outdated. I was going to talk to you about that because your place looks awesome. You did all the work yourself, right?"

"Yeah, it was actually fun," he says, nodding. "If you need help or just want me to do the work, let me know. I'm sure Wolf, Jagger, and even Axe would help if I asked."

"Axe is still in town? I thought he would have gone back now that all that drama is done with Duke and Roman." At his frown, I hurry to explain. "I don't mean to bring up bad memories, kid."

Watching Cadence still struggling to deal with his demons upsets me. He has been through so much in his life. Recently, both Cadence and Trinity revealed a similar past dealing with sexual abuse. Talk about a small world, as it turned out Duke, who is Cadence's stepdad, and Roman, who is Trinity's dad, not only knew each other but worked together with a gang of human traffickers. They also both abused Cadence violently and left him for dead. I still find it hard to believe these two kids found each other and fell in love. Their road to happiness has had some major bumps, but together with Hope, they seem to be finding their way.

Cadence just shrugs his shoulders. "Yeah, he's still around. I saw him the other day at Wolf's, hanging around Pru. That isn't going to happen if Wolf has anything to say about it. Rumor has it, Axe is worse than how I used to be and you know how protective Wolf is of his 'pack.'"

He starts laughing at his own pun and I just smile at his definition of Wolf's *volunteer work*.

It is good to know that Cadence is willing to help me, as my thoughts are to get the house updated and ready for Fern to come home. I just pray that happens soon. We finish our food and spend the night talking and getting together some ideas for the remodel. As the sun is coming up, Cadence gets up to leave.

"Cadence, thank you for being here tonight. Got no words to express how much I appreciated your company. You made it one of the best nights here so far, so thank you."

Nodding his head as he opens the door, he turns to

me. "Doc, you owe me nothing. We're family, and family is there when needed. I love you and Fern so I'll be here when I'm needed. Try to get some rest. We got the garage today. And, Doc," he says, bringing my attention to him. "Don't drink too many of those energy drinks. They can really fuck you up and do a ton of damage to your body."

Watching him leave, I think how right he is about those damn drinks. I also once again realize how lucky I am with the people in my life. Turning, I go back to sit at Fern's side and try to get a couple of hours of sleep.

(Fern)

As I watch Gabriel playing with little Hope, my heart clenches. He is a natural with babies, always has been. They just gravitate to him. Not sure if it is his size, gentle ways, or soft voice, but even in restaurants or stores if a baby is there, somehow they will grab Gabriel's attention. I feel the tightness in my chest, realizing I failed him as a wife. Even before when we tried to have a baby, but I just couldn't carry any of my pregnancies to term. After the last miscarriage, we talked and decided that we would not try again. It broke our hearts each time when I miscarried. We did discuss a baby surrogate and even went as far as to harvest my eggs and freeze them. Thank God we did ,because within months I was diagnosed with cancer. Sometimes I wonder if the in vitro shots caused the cancer but does it really matter at this point?

Hearing some cooing, I glance back to Baby Hope. As soon as I glance in that direction, her little eyes search around as if she is trying to find something or someone. When she looks in my direction, she stops and stares. Once again, the warmth goes through my body and I feel instantly at peace with barely any pain. I lie back in the bed and enjoy this moment. It seems the only time my body is relaxed totally is when that little baby is around me. I don't want to think like a crazy person and don't believe in all that wacky stuff people are always going on about—like superstitions or the supernatural—but for some reason there is a connection between Baby Hope and me. Dozing off, I hear Gabriel speaking to Hope like she is a child of four or five, not a baby three days old.

(Gabriel)

Watching Fern finally relaxing and falling into a much-needed nap, I gaze down into little Hope's dark eyes. They are just like her daddy's. Holding her in my arms, the ultimate feeling of peace comes over me. Each time she is in my presence I get the same emotion. Hope gives me a calm feeling and a serenity that I have never had anywhere else. This makes no sense to me intellectually as a grown man with some medical knowledge, and I don't get into all that new age stuff. I truly don't understand it, but do know that because of Hope we have a chance to get back to our most precious gift—our lives and Fern healthy.

Hugging her close to my chest, I whisper in her ear, "Thank you, little Hope, for giving my Fern a reason to fight. You are her little angel."

Feeling her wiggle closer as her little gloved hands press against my heart, she seems to get comfortable and then falls asleep on my chest, bringing me a sense of serenity. Holding this precious child to me, instantly I realize that God does listen to my prayers. Even when I'm asking for some kind of sign that we might have a chance at beating Fern's cancer. He didn't send a sign, nope, he sent down one of his beloved special angels. An angel who gave us not only the reason to believe, but also a one in a million chance at a stem cell match for the transplant.

And that angel is named Hope Powers.

CHAPTER FIVE

PRESENT ~ HORDE ~

(Des)

My day has gone to shit already. I've been on the phone with the bank for what seems like hours. Somehow, someone has tried to get into Gabriel and Fern's account from the charity ride and hack it. What the fuck is wrong with some people for Christ's sake? Thank God when I opened that account made is so only Gabriel, Fern, Cadence, or I can access it. So when someone online tried to make a transfer, the warning bells went off. Identity theft isn't what Doc and Fern need right now. I'm going to have to put a call in to Gabriel and explain what is going on. This could really affect them adversely if they don't get a handle on it right away. He'll need to address this immediately.

Reaching the counter, I look up and see Dee Dee's teenage son, Jagger, on the computer staring intently at something. A closer look tells me he is on a cancer site and looks to be taking notes.

"Hey, Jagger, what's up?"

He shoots me a glance then goes right back to what he is doing.

"Hi, Des. Mom is in the shop talking to the guys."

I walk around the counter and stand to his side. "Whatcha' doing, son?"

His entire body moves as it always does when I call him son. Jagger and Daisy have never had a male role model and are trying to get used to it. To top it off, that person would be me and being the alpha that I am, it's interesting how we're all figuring shit out and adapting. Jagger puts his pen down and turns toward me.

"I'm looking up what we are going to have to do for Fern once the procedure is done. Gosh, Des, there are so many things she can't do, eat, or be around for a while after. Daisy is looking up how the treatments will affect her physically and what can be done to make her more comfortable. Willow and Archie are working with Doc to make sure everything in the house is safe. They have been clearing away all of the closets and cabinets of all the harsh products, replacing them with environmentally safe stuff. We just found out that cat litter is a no, so when Fern gets home, the girls said they would take the cats to their apartment until it is safe for them to be returned. There is a lot to do, but we want Fern to be home recovering and safe. That's what Mom says anyway."

Instead of playing video games or messin' around with his friends on a day off of school, this kid is doing research for his mom's best friend. "I'm proud of you, Jagger," I say, lowering my head to him.

As he lifts his head quickly, he grins, I mean really big and at that moment I realize he's almost a grown man. How blessed we all are to have come together and formed a family of sorts. We always have each other's backs.

"So what am I supposed to be doing if y'all have it all covered?"

Jagger looks back to me and gives it to me straight. "According to what Mom said, you're responsible for Doc. It seems that he only listens to you and Cadence. Well, he listens to everyone because that's Doc, but he will only really take advice or help from you two. Cadence spent the night with him at Fern's bedside trying to keep his spirits up." Jagger leans in really close to me, looking around before he continues. "Cadence told Mom when he got back to the hospital after dropping Trinity and Hope off last night, that Gabriel, crap I mean Doc, was sitting in the chair next to Fern losing it. Mom asked Cadence what he did and he told her he grabbed on to Doc and told him to let it out. Des, um, what's going to happen if Fern doesn't make it?"

As he says those words, I can see Jagger struggling not to cry but he isn't succeeding. I put my hand on his shoulder and pull him to my side in a man hug.

"We ain't gonna think about that right now, Jagger, 'cause I'm getting good vibes from all of that shit, I mean stuff, we all heard regardin' the transplant shit." Jagger looks up at me with a smirk on his face.

"Don't be a smart-ass, kid. Your mom ain't around. Anyway, I did get a good feeling when Trinity announced the plan about Hope and the cell whatever transplant. We just have to wait and see. Until then, think positive thoughts, kid. Okay?"

Jagger nods, clearing his throat. "Des, have you noticed a difference in Daisy lately? Not sure, but something is going on and I'm worried. She never wants to hang out or even talk to me. I know some girls at school are being jerks to her, but I'm not sure if that is the problem. I do know these girls are the school's bullies and with Daisy being so shy, this could be why she's acting so weird lately."

"Jagger, with everything going on I haven't paid a lot of attention, but will talk to your mom and we'll look into this, okay?"

Once again he nods and pulls away, going back to the laptop for a second, then replies back, "Make sure you do, Des, I'm really worried about my sister." With my orders I nod my head, turn and walk to my office.

Sitting at my desk, I run my hands through my hair, frustrated that there really is nothin' we can do for Fern. The desolation of this fucked-up situation has my head throbbing. It seems like no matter how hard we all try to get Doc and Fern ahead; something is always pulling them back. Thank God the bank caught the threat. Gabriel will need to check to make sure no one stole either his or Fern's identity, because from what I hear that can be a total pain in the ass. And now, with Jagger's concerns, we have to look into what's going on with Daisy. Those little bitches better not be bullying my girl 'cause shit will hit the fan. Fuck, we never catch a break.

Lost in my own thoughts, I don't hear the door open or even hear her approaching until her hands start massaging my shoulders.

"What's the matter, Des? You sure are tense today. Jagger said he told you about what the kids are doing. They're really good kids, aren't they?"

Looking over my shoulder, my breath catches in my chest. *Damn, Dee Dee is a beautiful and sexy woman.* Right after that thought, I am overwhelmed with guilt as directly behind Dee Dee is Doc. Knowing what he's going through with Fern and that there's a chance she might not pull through, the reality hits me. As we head to the front office, I think about how Doc has never complained, whined, or played the poor me part. Ever. He has always been the go-to guy who would and has done anything for anyone who asks. How he can even maintain his composure to come into work and be around people amazes me. Taking a minute to look closely at him through the shop window, I realize that he doesn't look like himself. His face is flushed and his cheeks are kind of a ruby red color. But the thing I notice most is how he's profusely sweating and it isn't even hot in the garage. Standing up immediately, I gently slide Dee Dee over, walking through the shop door and get right in his face.

"Doc, what's wrong? Are ya feeling okay? Man, you do not look good." As he raises his head, I am shocked at how his eyes are dilated. His pupils are huge.

As my hand hits his shoulder, I can feel almost like a vibration coming off of him. Dee Dee comes to my side and looks, first at me, then glancing at Doc. I can tell her eyes see exactly what mine do. She comes to his other side and gently puts her hand around his waist. His eyes are shifting from both of us, as his lips get drawn and tight. He's building a wall around himself and it's almost like you can see it going up.

Something is definitely not right here and I'm not sure how to handle it. Doc's a grown man and was a medic in the service, so trying to pull one over on him ain't gonna happen. As my mind's trying to figure out the next steps, Doc shakes our arms off, heads out of the shop to my office, and plops in the chair in front of my desk, hands running through his hair impatiently. After a couple of minutes of this uncomfortable silence, he looks up at the two of us, and softly states almost to himself, "I fucked up. With everything going on the last couple of months, especially with Fern, her cancer, the charity ride, and work, I couldn't keep up. So I started to drink that Red Bull shit with the Five Hour Energy drink and take those pills to stay awake. Son of a bitch what are they called No Doze or Stay Awake or some shit. Got them at the Walmart when picking up some groceries. Then added any old pain prescriptions we had in the house. Well, needless to say they work, but now I can't stop taking them. Goddamn it, I should know better, but it has just been too much and there aren't enough hours in the day to fit it all in. To top it off, to calm down one night I took some old pain meds I had when I threw my back out. They worked, so now it seems like if I'm not taking one or the other, I'm drinking can after can of the energy drinks. I've fucked up and let Fern down."

He looks to his hands cupped on his lap, trying to avoid our eyes. Dee Dee rushes to him, grabbing his head and pulling him to her.

"Doc, if that's the worst thing you've done since all this started, no worries. We will help you with this," she tells him. "First, you need to go see Dr. Jazbowski and tell him what you are doing. I bet your blood pressure is sky-high. Maybe he can help you stop taking and drinking all that stuff. It isn't good for you, Gabriel, and Fern needs you right now." Softening her voice, Dee puts a smile on her face. "Man up and let's handle this. You are Fern's rock, so nothing can happen to you. She needs you. We good?"

Doc looks up at Dee and nods his head.

"Sorry to let you down, darlin'. My only concern, Dee Dee, is Fern, believe me. I just don't have the energy anymore."

"Sugar, can you go get both Doc and me a huge bottle of water from the kitchen?" I ask Dee.

She knows exactly what I'm doin' as she heads to the door, looking back. Doc can't see her and she gives me her million-dollar smile and a sassy wink as she heads out, closing the door behind her. I sit down next to Doc, struggling to find the words because I have no fuckin' idea what he is actually going through. His wife, lover, soul mate, possibly could die and there is nothing any of us can do. Realizing that he isn't coping with this well, I lay it out for him best I can.

"Doc, I have no words to make this better or even easier. All I do have is to remind you of my promise to be there for both Fern and you. You, Gabriel," his eyes shoot up to mine as I only use his given name when making a point, "are not alone in this and need to get that through your thick Irish skull. Let's get a schedule going so Fern's not alone at the hospital and you're not running yourself into the ground. 'Cause I'm telling ya, something happens to you, she's gonna be done."

Doc raises his head, looking confused. "You're her life and without you she has nothing to fight for so get your head out of your ass man, quit using that shit, and ask for help. Would ya please?"

As big of a man as Doc is, he seems to be coping the only way he knows how. Now he is trying to fight an addiction by himself.

I hate to add more to his plate, but need to let him know about the call from the bank. "Doc, got a call this morning from the bank. Someone was trying to transfer funds from your account to an internet account. One of the bank's auditors caught this and put a stop to it. We need to look at both Fern's and your credit reports to make sure no one has stolen your identity."

As I finish, Doc loses it, letting out a growl, and he jumps up, punching the wall directly next to my office door. Once, twice and finally a third punch as blood shoots from his torn knuckles.

"What the hell? How much more can I take of this shit, Des? Who the fuck would try to steal from us? All we have is the money from the charity ride."

Not knowing how to answer him, I'm thinkin'one person can only take so much and Doc is at his limit. There are no tears or sobbing, as I know Doc tries to do that in private. No, he'll struggle with this unbearable pain by himself, but I just can't stand by and watch. Grabbing his shoulder, I squeeze it, getting his attention.

"Doc, whatever you need I'm here for ya, man. We're family and family sticks together, so do what ya are gonna do, but two things first. Go see the doctor to control this shit you've been doing to your body, and share your burden with all of us. We're here for Christ's sake."

At this Doc sits straight up, cracking his neck, I guess trying to relieve the tension. Turning his gaze to look at me, I can see the agony and pain in his eyes.

"I know y'all are here for me and I appreciate it. Sometimes it just gets to be too much. I'm an idiot with all this shit I'm drinking and taking. Dee Dee is right. My blood pressure is sky-high. Going to see Dr. Jazbowski today and have to stop drinking that stuff and no more pills. But my body is craving that shit and it's going to be a battle not to fold and pop a pill or down one of those energy drinks. I'm gonna try to take you up on your offer and figure out a way to share the hospital visiting with everyone. That is killing me, Des. Sitting there all night, every night, watching her losing the battle as her spirit starts to dull. It is breaking my heart, and I can't do a damn thing about it. Thanks for being here for both of us. I couldn't pick a better man to call my friend, no, call brother, Des."

Knowin' Doc is done when he goes to stand, pulling away from me, I stand too. He doesn't say anything, and I just give him a head nod. Dee Dee walks in at that moment with the bottles of water, handing one to each of us. Doc thanks her and turns to leave, letting us know he is taking off early. As we watch him leave, I feel Dee fit herself into my side, releasing a sigh.

"Is he going to be okay, Des?"

Lookin' down at the woman I love, I sigh. "God, I hope so, babe, but only time will tell. All we can do is be here for him."

CHAPTER SIX

PAST ~ TIME FLIES BY ~

(Gabriel)

My thoughts go to my parents and how they lived their lives. It was all about the two of them all the time and us kids came in as afterthoughts. This made us grow up way too quickly and taking care of ourselves became second nature.

My siblings include older sister, Brannagh, my younger brother, Innis, and myself. With the verbal and physical arguments my parents had constantly, we tried to stay out of the way.

One particular brawl comes to mind. My pops had been drinking and he was one mean fucking drunk if I ever saw one. Mum made dinner, but it wasn't to his liking so he threw his plate at her. She proceeded to pick up the food and fling it back at him and the battle began. It wasn't anything we hadn't seen, but this time it went way too far as Pops threw my mum down the stairs. My sister immediately called the police. It was this incident that changed our lives. Pops was arrested and charged with a felony. Mum ended up with a brain injury and couldn't take care of us kids so we became wards of the state. I can't recall the last time I saw my sister or brother. We tried staying in touch, but for some reason life got in the way and we didn't. I got sick of being the one trying so hard to keep our family together when it seemed neither of them cared either way.

That is why when I rescued Fern back in high school, I finally realized what I wanted and she was it.

Hearing my name being called, I shake my head out of reminiscing about the past and walk toward the door. Someone grabs my arm out of nowhere. Looking down I see Katie, Des's ex. I don't even know it that's the right thing to even call her. They actually didn't even date. Anyway, I look from her hand on my arm to her eyes, then I raise my eyebrows. Personally, I never understood this woman. Waiting impatiently for her to let me go I see the nurse watching from down the hall in front of a patient room, I lose my patience.

"Hey, Katie. What's up?"

She squeezes my arm, then runs her hand up and down it softly as she gives me a soft smile that doesn't reach her eyes.

"Gabriel, just wanted to say hi and see if you were doing okay. I've heard through the grapevine Fern is yet again in the hospital so if there is *anything* I can do, don't hesitate to ask." Her other hand lands at my side as she steps closer to me.

As my mind catches up with what I'm seeing, I move my arm away from hers and step back. Did this awful bitch just make a pass at me? Really? While my wife is in the hospital fighting to live? Even knowing Des and I are friends from when they were together. No, wait. They weren't *together*. They were fuck buddies, nothing more. She would always be in my space if she were at the shop, Des's place, or the bar. I tried to avoid any contact with her when I knew she would be around. This though? Not happening. Ever.

"Thanks, Katie, for your concern, but all is good. Gotta run, but take care and I'll let Fern know you were asking about her."

I don't play that way and even if I were so low that I would consider fucking around on my wife, it wouldn't be with evil hearted Katie. There aren't many men in town that haven't had a taste of her. I prefer to go where it's not only clean, but also worthwhile. Besides, if you have Heaven, why would I want to take a chance of losing it for a brief hookup with her?

I can tell Dr. Jazbowski is disappointed in me after I explain the abuse with the energy drinks, the over-the-counter meds, along with the prescribed drugs. After he does the usual initial physical, he takes my blood pressure and then takes it again. From that I assume it is pretty high. He goes to his computer without a word to me and starts pounding on the keys.

"Okay, this is what I have," the doctor says, looking up at me. "You definitely have to quit the drinks. The caffeine levels in there with the amount you're drinking is very dangerous, Gabriel."

Hearing my given name I know he is serious.

"Your blood pressure is pretty high but I don't want to put you on any medication until we know it is necessary. This could be a side effect of the drinks and pills. No more pills either. I am prescribing you something to help you sleep."

I start to speak, but he silences me with a wave of his hand. "No arguing with me. Fern needs you to be there for her and you having a heart attack will not help either of you. So take one of these each night and you will sleep like a baby. I'm also prescribing you a very low dose anti-depressant medication. Before you say anything, Gabriel, you *are* taking both of these. Finally, you need to take care of yourself, as I can see you haven't been working out like regular. You've lost weight and your muscle mass has lessened. And I know you're thinking 'my wife is fighting cancer. Last thing I have time for is the gym.' Wrong! You need to stay healthy physically and mentally to get both of you through this."

Taking a breath, he intently watches me and then finishes. "You get me, Gabriel? This isn't a discussion. Go get these scripts filled and call it a day. Call Dee Dee or one of the others to go visit and take a night for yourself. Get a good meal, no alcohol, and a full night's sleep."

Thanking him, I head out of the office directly to my truck. Feeling like I have the weight of the world on my shoulders, I pull my phone out and dial Fern's room number. As she picks up, I take in a breath and let it out.

"Hey, sugar, how you doin'?"

Waiting for her reply, I lean back in my seat trying to get comfortable. Through the windshield Katie watches me from her car parked across the way. That's weird. Why is she still here? Not my problem and thank God it isn't Des's any longer. Listening, I hear Fern.

"Gabriel, did you hear me? What did the doctor tell you? I want you to stay home tonight and have a night just for you. Okay? Can you do that for me, husband, please? I am worried about you. I need you more than ever, Gabriel. I can't do this without you."

I hear the sniffling through the phone, letting me know she is crying.

"Sugar, now come on, no need to cry. I'll stay in tonight and just relax. Anything for you, but please don't, sugar, don't cry. You know that you crying tears me apart."

As we continue our conversation, I start the truck and head to the pharmacy to take care of what I have to. We finish as I pull into a spot. "You are my *treasure*, sugar. Know this and never forget. I'll call you later on, okay?"

Saying our goodbyes, I head into the store unaware of the eyes following me as I walk in.

CHAPTER SEVEN

PRESENT ~ TIMELINE FOR TREATMENT ~

(Gabriel)

Sitting here on the bed with Fern, listening to all that Julie is sharing with us gives me heart palpitations so I can imagine how my wife is feeling. She has had the chemotherapy and radiation before, but never to this extent or as a pre-treatment for a stem cell transplant. From the explanation Nurse Julie is giving to all of us, they are essentially going to kill everything in Fern's body to get it ready for the transfer of stem cells from Hope, which they then hope will attach, take, and then flourish.

Finally realizing that this is some serious shit, I knew that but hearing it makes it real, I start to feel the anxiety build in my chest. It's times like this I really jones for an energy drink with a couple of pills. But that isn't going to happen anymore. I've got to stay strong.

I am listening intently as the nurse, Julie, goes

through what will be happening the next couple of weeks and months. As we listen, she pulls a dry board out and starts to show Fern exactly how this will proceed. First and foremost, they will be putting in a new central line, which Julie calls a Hickman catheter. This line will tunnel under Fern's chest to decrease the chance for infection to enter the bloodstream. The line is where the chemotherapy is going to be given, along with antibiotics, blood, and IV fluids. I didn't realize that Fern would not be coming home, but starting the treatments immediately. In fact, as we're speaking, the doctor begins the process of ordering everything and moving this right along. Julie continues explaining that Fern will be in the hospital at least for a month to receive the chemotherapy. They also plan on doing something called consolidation therapy monthly to make sure the leukemia cells are leaving the body. Since Fern has already had chemo not that long ago, they're going to give her the much stronger one, for fourteen to twenty-one days, prior to the transplant to basically destroy the immune system and try to kill any remaining leukemia cells.

Julie takes a much-needed break for a breath, as everyone is looking a bit green around the gills knowing the grueling schedule that Fern will be following. I am personally worried about her being able to handle all these different treatments prior to the transplant. Scanning the room, meeting everyone else's concern, I get Julie's attention.

"Is there no other way besides all of the chemo,

Julie? Fern has been getting treatment on and off for the last couple of years, and as you can see, it's taking its toll."

Before I can keep going, Fern lifts her fragile hand, reaching and grabbing mine.

"Gabriel, let her finish and don't worry. I am ready for this. I've told you this is going to be the fight of my life and plan on doing whatever it is so I can get Baby Hope's stem cells in me and pray they take."

Clearing her throat, Julie goes on, "So once we are ready for the transplant that becomes day zero, which is the day Hope's stem cells will be transplanted into Fern. This procedure to infuse Hope's cord blood into Fern will take approximately one to two hours. Now, it generally does take quite a while for the engraftment, or transplanted blood, to take over and for the bone marrow to begin making healthy cells. Since it's cord blood, it can take anywhere between twenty-four to forty-two days to take. Now between blood cells, CBC (complete blood count), neutrophils, the white cells that fight infection, and platelets that help control bleeding, it can take up to eight weeks for them to graft. So, to give you an idea it can be between thirty and a hundred days before Fern will be allowed to go home, and that depends on the engraftment and if there are any complications of infection. If discharged at the thirty-day window, the patient will be released to a facility close to the hospital so they can return back for daily blood tests and physical therapy. Also, this gives the patient a chance to get acclimated to being out of the hospital but not home yet. Remember this is very intense and not only physically, but psychologically as well. Fern would stay at the outpatient facility for anywhere from a couple weeks to a couple of months as the tests would be a couple times a week to weekly, or every other week as time goes by. Does anyone have any other questions?" Julie asks. "I think this has tired Fern out, so I recommend everyone give her some time to rest. She is going to need you all in the near future, so let's give her and Gabriel some time to absorb all this information."

I glance around as everyone gets ready to leave, waiting his or her turn to kiss, hug, or just squeeze my wife's hand in support. As the room empties, all the guys in the hall wait their turns to come in and support my Fern in this next fight for life. Seeing the abundance of people waiting to come in, it hits me how very fortunate we are. Fern and I might not have a lot of material wealth but looking at the people here to support us, we are wealthy in ways words can't explain.

Feeling someone stop directly in front of me, I look down into Daisy's amber eyes. Eyes just like her momma's.

"Doc, I wasn't being nosy. I just ,I love her so much..." Her eyes fill up and flow over with fresh tears running down her face.

As Dee Dee and Des rush to pull her away, I grasp Daisy by the shoulder, pulling her close. "Sweetheart, knowing that you care that much for my Fern fills my heart with joy. Never apologize for caring or loving, young lady. Understand?" She nods as I continue, "Fern has a way about her that makes everyone love her like I do. She is going to need that so I'm asking, no, begging you to make time for her and let her know you care. That will mean the world to both of us. Can you do that for me?"

She answers with a very timid, "Yeah, totally, Doc, I can."

Bringing her in for a hug I quietly continue, "Daisy, both Fern and I know something is going on with you." She jerks her head up, looking at me. "Whatever is going on with you, know there are people who care deeply for you so don't think you're alone. You get what I'm telling you, sweetie?"

She stares at me for a bit then replies back, "Yeah, Doc, I get what you are saying." As she finishes, both Dee Dee and Des arrive behind her. Seeing Des watching both of us, I mouth to him "later" then gesture to Daisy so he knows what it's about.

"We're all good, aren't we, Daisy?"

Daisy smiles up at me through her tears then turns to her mother as they walk out, Dee Dee squeezes my hand as she goes by. Watching them leave, I notice Daisy seems to have lost quite a bit of weight, which she didn't have to lose in the first place. I add Daisy to my list of things to worry about. Glancing at Des, he waits until they are gone.

"Anything you need, Doc, and I mean anything, just let me know. Dee Dee is going to work out a rotation so Fern is never here alone, if that works for you."

He gives me a fist punch to the shoulder and heads out after his family.

After what seems like hours, Fern and I are finally alone. She shifts in her bed so I can get my bear of a body next to hers after kicking my shoes off. Pulling her close, feeling her breath on my chest brings me such peace, I just take it in for a minute. God, I can't lose this. It will break me. I'd never be the same. As if my wife can read my thoughts, she squeezes my side.

"Gabriel, remember this is out of our hands. No matter what, you will go forward and move on. I will give this my best, but you need to start to accept that if this doesn't work, my fight will be over. Please. You need to come to terms with that." Not wanting to get in that mood of hopelessness, I continue to hold her to me, sharing my body heat with her cold, fragile body.

"Sugar, you know my thoughts on that subject, so let's not go there. I'll continue to do anything humanly possible to make sure that you, no, we beat this thing and get back to what we do best—livin' our lives. Now I don't want any sass back from you. Let's just enjoy this and relax as we have a crap load of stuff coming our way pretty quick."

Her breathing relaxes and slows down and I know the instant she falls asleep. Wishing and knowing it will be a while for my body to shut down and drift off, I hold my wife close to me, envisioning all kinds of scenarios in our future. Once the cancer is finally gone, knowing in the back of my mind that there are no guarantees in this process, maybe then we can get back to living our lives. What's worse for me is there is nothing I can do except sit by and wait, just like everyone else.

Getting out of the bed, I reach for my coat so I can get my nighttime medication as I can feel the start of the shakes from the caffeine withdrawals start. Dr. Jazbowski was right. This isn't going to be easy, but these drugs are helping me, so I'm going to keep on this path. I think back to when I told Fern about this. She was so upset until I told her that it was my screwup, not hers. I chose to take those pills and drinks to keep me up. I told her that instead I should've asked for some help, knowing that everyone would have changed their schedules to give me a hand. I'm glad that it's out in the open. This hasn't been easy, showing my weakness, and I know I was really getting hooked, but telling Fern and dealing with it was the right thing to do. Fighting back will be hard, but worthwhile. Each day the need for that shit is getting a little bit less, but if I'm honest, coming off of this stuff is really hard. I'm hopeful it will get easier with time.

Going back to the bed, I make sure Fern is covered up as I once again pull the recliner close and get settled for the night. I don't feel comfortable sleeping in the small hospital bed with Fern, so usually I lay down with her until she falls asleep. Stretching out on my makeshift bed, I let the meds take over and fall into a deep sleep.

Time doesn't wait for anyone and that in itself has me ready to pull my hair out. We are in week two or three, I'm not even sure anymore, of Fern's intense chemotherapy treatment to kill everything so the stem cell transplant can be done. Watching her day in and day out is tearing my heart and soul out as Fern struggles to keep up a good front. To try and give her something to look forward to, I've started to work on our home. Never did I think it would turn into the project it has, but it also has given everyone something to do that makes our lives feel normal. Whatever the hell that is. As I am getting dressed, I hear the weak doorbell so buttoning my jeans, I grab a T-shirt, and head to the door to see who the hell is here so early.

What the hell is *she* doing here? I don't need any trouble and with Des and Dee Dee on the way to help me with the choices for Fern's dream kitchen, this has to be handled quickly. She needs to be gone before they get here.

Unlocking the door, I look at the woman with a casserole dish in her hands and immediately get a bad feeling. A shiver runs up my back warning me to watch myself. Shit, can she cook *and* do...I shouldn't go there.

"Hey, Doc. I made too much of my homemade sauce so I hope you like spaghetti and meatballs," Katie spits out without taking a breath. Seeing her nervousness puts me on high alert, especially since she had been Des's "piece of ass" for years, his words. Not to mention it didn't end well at all when he decided to go after Dee Dee finally.

Katie was a terror for months to both of them, making life in our small town very uncomfortable until she seemed to move on. Knowing way too much about Des's relationship, I can barely look her in the eyes. He didn't speak highly of her.

"Well, thanks, sweetie. That's very kind of you. Let me take that and get it in the fridge. Thanks for dropping it by. Have a good day."

Grabbing the dish, I turn with the intention of getting this in the fridge so I can get ready for my day. Just as Des had promised, Dee Dee has worked out a schedule for the hospital so not only is Fern never alone, but it gives me time to get shit done here before she is released. Thinking on that, my heart wants one thing but my head knows it will be a while before she walks through that front door.

Sighing, I go to the fridge to find it packed already. Shifting shit around I shove her dish in. With my back to Katie, I don't have a clue of her intentions until too late. I feel her warm body press into mine hard, as her hands immediately reach for my crotch. She gets my zipper halfway down before I grab her hands. Trying to get her off of me without hurting her is a struggle. Feels like she has twelve hands not just two. She's out of control as we fight over my damn zipper. One of her hands keeps reaching to pull the tab down farther as her other hand squeezes my cock through my jeans.

The thought of her hands on me, gags me. Then my nightmare gets much worse.

"What in the fuck is going on? Bitch, move away from Doc now unless ya want to deal with me."

Pushing her away from me, I immediately pull my zipper back up, as she watches me, eyes blazing fire. Something immediately changes in her and I see the sparkle in her eyes. Here comes trouble. Turning away from me she puts her hand on her hip, glaring at both Des and Dee Dee.

"What's the matter, Des? Not getting it enough at home? You jealous that poor Doc here is getting some affection with Fern unable to take care of her man?"

As a rage I never knew before takes over, I roughly grab Katie by her upper arm, turning her to face me. As my body physically shakes from uncontrollable fury, I fix my eyes to hers.

"Never, and I mean *never*, do I want to hear Fern's name out of your mouth, Katie. You get me? Now I don't know what the fuck game you're playing at, but I'm not interested. Not now and not ever, so get the hell out of my house and take your food with you. You should be ashamed of yourself knowing Fern is fighting for her life. Go play your asinine games with someone else."

I slam the casserole dish in her hands, but she doesn't hold it and the Corning Ware crashes to the floor, spaghetti and meatballs all over.

"Doc, you can lie to yourself, but I felt how much you wanted to be with me. Your hard cock throbbing in my hand was pushing to get out for some much-needed release. So keep avoiding the truth, but know that if you need me, all you have to do is call me. As for you two, go fuck yourselves."

Pushing Dee Dee out of her way, Katie walks right out the door past Wolf and Cadence as they are walking up to the house. The disgusted looks on their faces show how much they dislike the woman, but she gives them a huge smile as she walks by them, sashaying her hips as if she doesn't have a care in the world.

In the house, watching everything like it's a terrible movie, I sit down at my kitchen chair, head in my hands.

I hear Cadence's voice before I see him. "What was that fucking whore doing in Fern's house, Doc?" Seeing me bent over the table, Cadence touches my shoulder. "Doc, what's wrong?" Hearing the concern in his voice, I lift my head as he continues to react to the tension in the room.

"What the fuck did you do, Doc? Tell me you didn't fuck that bitch in Fern's home. What the fuck's the matter with you for Christ's sake?" Cadence spits out.

Feeling not only his disapproval but also his hurt for my wife, I try to explain but am just too shocked myself. Why did my body start to react to her like that as I don't even like the woman? I know it has been forever since Fern and I were intimate as that is the last thing on her mind. We've even talked about, or I should say Fern talked about, some stupid idea that she called a "hall pass." I had no idea what that was until she explained that she knew I had needs and if I wanted to get some relief, she would understand. I was blown away thinking she was reading way to many of those books on her Kindle, because I took my vows seriously and never even thought of another woman, no matter how long it has been. Yes, I have needs, but I take care of them myself when the need is too much, while thinking of my wife no one else.

But Fern had to tortured both of us with this conversation until I had to tell her to stop it. I had no interest in sex with other women. Fern then shocked the shit out of me by grabbing my jeans and unzipping them to give me a quick hand job in the hospital room. Feeling her soft, petite hand gripping my cock, I instantly went hard. As I panicked that a nurse might walk in, she softly squeezed and put pressure on me. The tension washed away as she increased her grip, going up and down on my length. Not knowing what to do, I stood there like an idiot as my sassy sick wife managed in no time at all to get me off.

"Gabriel," she'd said once I'd come, "I know that this has been extremely difficult for you, so don't be upset. I need to connect and be close with you whenever I can. I love you always."

Who would have thought a slip of a woman could bring me to my knees? Hearing my name I realize that I had drifted from the present. Dee Dee asks if I am all right and I blink to clear my head, nodding in the general direction of her voice.

"Doc, you need to be very careful. That woman is a sick bitch. She'll not stop until she gets what she wants. Please listen to me as I've been on the receiving end of that."

Clearing my throat, I take them all in and try to explain, "The doorbell rang and she brought some food, so as I went to put it in the fridge, she followed me closely and one thing led to another and that's what you walked in on. It was her pursuing me, not the other way, I swear. God, what an asshole I am. Fern lies in the hospital fighting for her life while I am being manhandled by Katie. What the fuck was I thinking? Now I have to tell Fern what happened."

I hear several "noes" as they all look at me like I'm nuts. Wolf finally steps forward. "Doc, don't tell your wife about this incident. Trust me, it will not go well, especially since it's Katie, who all the women hate because of the on and off again shit with Des. Take it for what it is and move on."

Having Wolf's eyes watching me so closely, even with everyone else right there, I feel the emotions crawling up my spine. Not knowing how to control them and not let loose in front of them all, especially the guys, I try to suck it up until I feel someone walk right up to me, pull me from the chair and wrap his arms around me holding me tightly. Hearing his voice breaks me as my eyes start to leak wet. Cadence puts it out there.

"Doc, you're the best man I know. Don't overthink this. Don't torture yourself and just let this shit go. Life is way too fucking short, as we all know, and you have so much on your plate it amazes me that you can even function somewhat normally." Squeezing me he continues, "Sometimes life takes us down that road less traveled and we can either complain or look around, find the beauty there momentarily, and then get the fuck out and get on with life. That's what you have to do. Take it with a grain of salt. Don't let that bitch upset you, and more importantly, upset Fern. We good now, Doc? 'Cause we got a fuckin' full day ahead of us."

Wiping my eyes, I look into his almost black eyes, which seem to be so much wiser lately, and just shake my head. Dee Dee comes by with some coffee and we all sit around the table going over the plans for Fern's dream kitchen as I try to forget what transpired with Katie, hoping it never happens again, but knowing her, this trouble is just starting.

CHAPTER EIGHT

PRESENT ~ UNCERTAINTY ~

(Fern)

Gosh, I have never felt so bad in my entire life. My entire body hurts so badly from the chemo treatments, and my stomach can't seem to hold down anything I put in my mouth. And my mouth is filling up with those sores that hurt so much I don't even want to eat. I know everyone is worried about me, but I barely have enough to get me through each day, so I have nothing left to try and make them all feel better. I hate they worry so much.

The nurses have been wonderful, but I can tell they are concerned by the way they are acting and making extra trips into my room. As I am thinking this, Julie walks in, a small smile on her face. I see her run through her daily routine, looking at each machine, mentally recording what they tell her about me and where I am at this moment in time. Seeing her staring at the machine and her notes as her eyes look at the results then me, and then back again at her notes, I feel my body trembling with fear. Now what is the problem? I've never wanted to be a *poor me* type, but these last couple of weeks have been really rough. The chemo is literally kicking my butt, and to top it off, I noticed my hair is not only thinning but also starting to fall out in chunks. This depresses me as it was just starting to look normal again.

Looking up at Julie, I inquire, "What's up, Julie? You look concerned."

She holds up her finger to silence me as she goes to the computer to record all the stats. Reaching for the blood pressure cuff she softly asks, "Feeling okay today, Fern? It looks like your pressure is low, that is why I'm going to take it manually. Could be that automatic cuff not reading correctly. Give me your arm for a sec, will you, hon?"

The cuff tightens as Julie pumps it and I am suddenly light-headed. The room starts to spin. Hearing her voice as if she is far away, the last thing my eyes pick up is Gabriel's panicked tremble in his voice

"What is going on? Julie, talk to me! Fern stay with me, sugar. Come on please, Fern, stay with me."

I feel like I am drifting on clouds with no pain or worries, my body is light and my mind is free. I feel weightless as my body and mind drift aimlessly. Subconsciously I realize, with a soft touch on my arm, that I am starting to wake up. I can't understand what's being said around me. Hands run up and down my arm, squeezing my fingers every time they are held by someone's hand. Slowly my senses come back to me, first smell and by that I can smell Gabriel's unique scent close by. It reminds me of being in a forest as I can find hints of evergreen, musky vanilla, and his own special scent.

Then my hearing clears and I actually hear my husband praying for me to wake up. There is total fear in his voice, and finally my eyelids open as I try to focus and make out the shapes around me. Julie and Gabriel are to my right while Des and Dee Dee are to my left. All faces are concerned, but Gabriel's is very pale, his face drawn with worry and something else I've never seen on his face before. Fear.

Julie reaches for my hand to take my pulse.

"Dee Dee, go to the front desk and please have the nurse page Dr. Davids immediately for me." As she leaves, Julie lightly taps my hand for my attention.

"Fern, what are you feeling at this moment? Tell me everything, okay, honey?"

Taking a breath, I start to answer her but the voice I hear doesn't even sound like me. It is weak and broken. "I'm very cold, vision is blurry, and my cognitive brain isn't working right. I am off center, so to speak. Why, Julie? What's going on with me?" I search for my husband, catching his gaze. "Gabriel, what's going on and why do you look so guilty?"

Immediately his eyes shoot to Des who, if I wasn't watching, I wouldn't have seen the small nod of his head. Des continues to look Gabriel's way and mouths to my husband, "No fucking way" as Gabriel looks from him to me a couple of times.

Trying to sit on the bed, Gabriel reaches for my hand. "Sugar, I have no idea what you're talking about. All I know is when we came in you were white as a ghost and passed out before we could get to you. I've been worried sick about you, but Julie was stellar. She kept calm and waited for you to wake up. Need anything, Fern?"

Shaking my head, I know in my heart something isn't right here, but don't have enough energy to even pursue it right now. I put this in the back of my head to be revisited later when my head is clear.

Dr. Davids and Dee Dee enter the room and Des immediately pulls his wife to him, whispering in her ear. Her eyes shoot to me but move quickly on when she sees me watching them. Her eyes then land on Gabriel as his shoot to the floor, avoiding her inquisitive glare. Something doesn't seem right. I can't put my finger on it. Or maybe it's the massive amount of drugs I'm on making me imagine things. I'm not sure.

Dr. Davids gets my attention with some general questions and after a thorough exam orders some tests. A look passes between the doctor and nurse as she leaves the room. He turns in the general direction of the bed where everyone is standing.

"I'm not sure, but I think you might be bleeding internally, Fern. That is why I have ordered the tests and some blood work. We'll know as quickly as the tests can be done. Do not panic, as this is a side effect of such intense chemotherapy. Sit tight and I'll be back shortly."

As he leaves the sudden tension in the room becomes almost unbearable. Feeling horrible and watching the three of them avoid my eyes, I finally just ask, "What's going on, Gabriel? Might as well just tell me because it's obvious that something happened. Just spit it out so we can move on."

My husband's body tenses up, as he quietly replies, "Not now, Fern. You have enough on your plate. Everything is fine. We'll talk later."

Dee Dee looks up and I catch her gaze. What I see sends a cold shiver down my spine. She can tell that I know it isn't good, but just when I get ready to ask again, she shakes her head slightly, her eyes begging me not to.

After what seems like forever, Dr. Davids and Julie are back in my room with the results.

"The problem is that the chemotherapy is breaking down your cells, which in turn leads to bleeding in your belly. We are going to put you on some medication and watch you closely. Hopefully, your body will absorb the blood. We are skipping tomorrow's chemo treatment and giving your body some time off to rest. We will be pumping you with platelets to assist in rebuilding your system. Does that sound good, Fern?"

I just nod my head, acknowledging what he has

told me. Gabriel holds my hand but I can feel the clammy touch, which isn't normal for him. I wonder if it's from the withdrawal of the drugs and drinks he was abusing or whatever has him feeling guilty. We definitely need to talk and soon. Once the doctor leaves again, everyone settles down and we play some gin rummy to pass the time.

A few hours later, Des and Dee Dee leave. Gabriel and I are finally alone. He removes his shoes as he has done every night since I was admitted, probably intent on lying with me until I fall asleep, but I need to know what is bothering him.

"Gabriel, please tell me what is going on. My mind is running around in all directions. I worried about you."

He sits in the chair and grabs my hands. "Sugar, I don't want to upset you. That's why I don't want to talk about this shit. I feel bad enough for both of us and knowing if we speak about this it's just going to hurt you, which I swore never, would happen. Can't we drop it and enjoy each other's company tonight?"

I can't help the tremors that overtake my body. "Gabriel, we never keep anything from the other, even if it's going to hurt. That was our promise to each other, so please just get it out."

He grabs his head, running fingers through his long hair. When he looks up, I see the pain in his eyes.

"I was home this morning, waiting for the Horde to come over and look at the designs for the kitchen like we talked about. Someone was at the door and when I opened it, it was Katie."

He notices my small gasp, but continues, "She brought over a casserole and as I went to put it in the fridge with all the others, she followed me and tried to ... Shit, sugar, don't know how to say this, but she manhandled me. I didn't ask for it or want it, but Des and Dee Dee walked in and saw Katie with her hands all over me." He lowers his head. "I'm so sorry, Fern. God, I don't know how this happened."

Feeling beyond jealous and wanting to pull that blonde she-devil's hair out, which the thought shocks me, I take a couple of breaths. "Gabriel, look at me, please. When you had her in your arms did you enjoy it? Want it? Feel amorous toward her?" I wait, holding my breath for his answer.

When he replies, what he tells me will be with me for the rest of my life. "Sugar, I've never touched another woman since we became serious, when I first got back from the service. With you being sick, I haven't thought about sex in a long while. No, take that back, I've thought about all the times we have had sex, made love, or as you used to say, did the nasty."

Hearing him say that actually brings a smile to my lips as I softly giggle. "Not gonna lie to you either, Fern, when she first touched me I was shocked, and my body didn't respond. Then when she grabbed my dick, to my utter surprise it started to react and get hard. Well, semi-hard." As I let out a painful moan Gabriel tries to grab my hand, but I don't want to touch him now. She touched him. My Gabriel, my husband, my best friend, that witch—no—she deserves to be called a bitch.

He continues, "Sugar, got no words that can change what happened. I didn't go looking for it and I stopped her once I was over the shock. You have every right to be mad or even pissed off, but please remember that we took vows that I've honored all these years. You're my sunshine in the morning, my calm during the day, and you bring me peace at night being able to hold you in my arms. Please, don't be upset. You shouldn't have any stress right now. I'm sorry, sugar."

Reaching for his hand, I squeeze it as I look into those emerald eyes that shine with love, so I give him what he needs.

"No need to apologize, my love. You didn't do anything wrong. Thank you though for sharing it with me and not hiding it. Come here, Gabriel. Lie down with me. I want to feel you next to me."

As my husband holds me tight, running his hands down my back, massaging away the day's tension, I can still feel the tension in his body. Right before I fall asleep, I mumble softly, "Gabriel Murphy, I love you with my entire being."

He squeezes me tight and whispers against my ear, "Fern, you're my lifelong treasure. I love only you, sugar."

CHAPTER NINE

PRESENT REFLECTING ~ REMEMBERING OUR FIRST TIME ~

(Gabriel)

The last couple of days I've been feeling like a total failure. As my wife lies in that hospital bed day in and day out, there's nothing I can do for her. Her hair is coming out in clumps, and she asked me to bring the clippers tonight so we can get rid of her hair all at once. I have to go get her some scarfs to wear, even though she didn't ask for them. But that is Fern. She never wants or asks for anything for herself, but will give her time—not to mention her last dollar for anyone in her life.

Watching her face fall when I told her about Katie broke my heart. That was the one time I actually thought about not being honest because I wanted to protect her. I'll never forget the look on her face, even though she didn't say it, after hearing how my body betrayed both of us, I failed her as a husband for the first time in our marriage. Damn Katie to hell. Why did she have to choose me to try and make Des jealous? Like that's ever going to happen because my friend is so totally in love with Dee Dee. Anyway, enough about that bitch Katie. I need to get my head out of my ass and in the right space. I've a plan and need help from everyone, in order to surprise Fern. She needs some uplifting and that is my job as her husband. I have put the calls out already and they should be arriving shortly.

As I sit waiting for their arrival, my mind goes back in time. It has been doing this quite frequently lately. Getting up, I go to our family room and drop down onto my recliner, looking at our wedding picture on the wall. Fern was such a shy, quiet girl, but she was also a beauty. I remember the first time I kissed her and she grabbed onto me like a monkey, which shocked the crap out of me. Even though we were hanging out, in the beginning she was too young and naïve, while I was a young guy who had raging hormones in my body.

My virginity was lost to a senior cheerleader before I knew Fern was going to be it for me. By that time I had been around the block, so to speak, as much as a kid my age could be, but once she fell into my arms, my body was willing to wait for her and only her. We started slow as she was so introverted that I didn't want to scare her. But after that first kiss, we took things as they came. We'd been together for the first three years of high school when I made it to second base. And man, was that something. Never had I been so nervous and just touching Fern made me blow in my jeans. Thank God she had no idea, as she had never been with anyone in that way. She would tentatively touch my chest, running her fingers across my nipples or down to my stomach, and my breath would catch in my throat. As we grew closer, she began to explore a bit more. When she finally reached for me, over my jeans, watching her eyes grow in shock actually made me laugh, which embarrassed her, but we got through it. As time went on, our relationship started to change as not only were we in love, but being young we were hungry for each other. Never did I rush or push her. My hand got a workout back in those days. But my Fern was worth it and still is.

When we finally decided that it was time to take our relationship to the next level. I planned for weeks. We both were still in high school, senior year, and lived with our parents. I didn't want our first time in the back of a car or truck, so I had to really think about it.

Finally, it came to me in my science class. My friend's parents had a cabin by the lake, which would set the scene perfectly. He asked his folks if we could use it as my brother and I wanted to go fishing. They said we could as long as we didn't wreck the place. So once the place was secured then I needed to make it perfect. That night I took Fern to dinner at the nicer family restaurant in town, then drove out to the cabin. I told her to give me a minute and went in to put the finishing touches together. When I went back out to get Fern, she was sitting on the ground next to the car, knees to her chest, trembling. Getting down with her, worried that something happened, she looked up with tears in her eyes.

"Fern, what's wrong, sugar?"

She shook her head as tears flew everywhere. "Gabriel, once we do this are you going to break up with me because you finally got...you know? If so, then I don't want to go all the way because I don't ever want to lose you."

I grabbed and pulled her close. "We don't have to do anything you don't want to. Your parents think you are spending the night with a friend, not that they care either way, and mine are at some party so we can just go in and spend time together. No pressure, okay?"

Helping her up, we walked into the cabin and she stopped in the doorway. During the day I'd brought flowers and had them around the room, along with some candles flickering throughout the small cabin.

"Go sit down, sweetie. I'll get us something to drink." After starting a fire, we sat together relaxing, talking, and just enjoying each other's company. Knowing we were both nervous, I didn't want her to feel like she had to do this, I never made a move toward her. I just held her close as the night went on and we talked about everything—our classes, what we wanted to do after we graduated, and college.

As the night passed, Fern moved closer to me and

started to touch me tentatively. As things started to heat up, I gave her another chance to back out. "Baby, we don't need to do this. I love just having you close."

Her reply was to pull my head down and softly press her lips to mine. My body immediately exploded with all the feelings she brought to the surface. I watched her every move and reaction, and by the time we made it to the bedroom we were both gasping. Never had I ever felt these intense emotions. I'd been with some other girls but that was more of a physical thing. Fern owned my heart. Gently removing her clothes as she blushed, I saw perfection in front of me. *Her body was made for me*, I thought as I removed my own, watching her eyes. As I dropped my boxers, her eyes got huge as her mouth opened in an O. Looking down at my cock then back at me, panic and even fear showed on her face.

"Gabriel, oh my God, will that even fit in me? I mean, you know you seem to be really...big. I even would go as far as to say huge."

I laughed softly as I started to touch her, trying to gauge what she liked and didn't. She became a wiggly worm as everywhere I touched her made her giggle or gasp. As I ran my hand down her soft flat stomach, reaching for the prize between her legs, she put her hand on mine squeezing.

"I trust you totally, Gabriel, and I love you."

With those words, I felt a calm come over me as I touched, squeezed, and played Fern's body until she was wet and willing. When I pushed my fingers into her core, she bucked up and then down, not sure what to do. Continuing to pump in and out gently as my other hand touched that bundle of nerves, I had my Fern slowly going crazy. When I felt her body tense, I pushed my two fingers in and pinched her clit as she had her first orgasm. Watching her lose control and give in to the pure beauty of this moment, I knew that it was time. Reaching to the nightstand where I had condoms stacked up, I grabbed one, ripped it open, and put it on carefully. I also grabbed the small bottle of lube, rubbing it up and down my condom-covered cock, knowing this would make it a bit more comfortable for her first time. As Fern went to grab me, I moved back. She looked lost until I explained

"Fern, I am so close that if you touch me it will be over before we start."

She smiled slowly and shook her head.

"Honey, I'm going to go slow, but from what I hear this is gonna hurt you so tell me if it is too much, okay?"

As I lined my cock up at her entrance, I leaned down and started to kiss her. As she kissed me back, my hips started to move as I entered her and pushed forward. At first, she accepted it and spread her legs to accommodate me until I pushed up against her hymen. Her breath started to come in small gasps while her hands were grabbing my hips and I couldn't tell if she was pulling me or pushing me away. I stopped immediately, looking deep into her eyes.

"Fern, we can still stop. Just say the word, honey,

because you know I'd never hurt you. Never, Fern, I promise." She took in a deep breath, ran her hands up and down my back, and then tentatively touched my butt. Giving her all the time she needed, I could feel my cock leaking precum into the condom as I was so ready, but this wasn't about me at all, it was about her.

The first time has to be special especially for the girl, or more like a girl like Fern. As she was touching me and rubbing up against me, her face flushed as she also rubbed her perky breasts on my body. I felt her walls clenching me inside and she wrapped her legs around mine, hanging on for dear life.

Looking back at her I asked, "Okay, Fern?"

She gently pushed on my butt, lowering her eyes slightly asking me, "Can you move some, Gabriel? It feels good but I need you to move."

Knowing those next couple of minutes weren't going to be fun for her, I braced myself above her and in one smooth hip movement I planted myself totally in her, as I heard her small scream of pain. She tried to push me off, but I held her close, staying perfectly still, feeling her body accommodating for my size and length. After a couple of minutes I moved tentatively and when she matched me, we started to move then find our rhythm. Feeling the pressure building and running up and down my spine as my balls started to tighten, wanting to make it just as good for her, I placed my hand between us, tweaking her love button, adding pressure back and forth over it. As I felt the wetness from her body covering mine, it drove me crazy.

Between her heat, wetness, and innocent movements I knew I was done.

"Sugar, I'm gonna come but I need you to go first. Just feel me, Fern. My body covering you, my cock in your warm pussy all tight and wet for me. Come on, baby, let it go. Come for me."

Feeling her legs tighten around my ass, I started to put pressure back on the button filled with nerves as I began to seriously rotate and shift my hips, trying to find and hit all the sensitive spots in her.

Fern's breath was coming in gasps as she whispered, "Gabriel, please talk to me like you just did. It really makes me hot." I looked down to see her face was a beautiful shade of pinkish red from her revealing she likes dirty talk.

"Oh, baby girl, you have no idea what you just opened up. I love the feel of your tight wet pussy around my hard cock. Come on, girl, let go for me..." Just then her entire body tightened for a minute or so, then she immediately relaxed as she moaned her release into my neck. Knowing she was there I pushed in one, two, three times, and then held it there as I reached that point and felt myself let loose.

As we both came back to earth, I looked at the naïve young girl in my arms with shock on my face.

"So my little Fern likes dirty talk, huh?"

She tried to hide her face but I grabbed her chin, lifting her head.

"No, Fern, we never hide from each other. The only way this works is trust and honesty always.

Nothing to be embarrassed about, sugar, 'cause I plan to know this hot little body as well as I know my own."

As I smiled down at her, she gave me a shy smile but her eyes were twinkling.

"Got to get rid of this condom, Fern, be right back." As I shifted and moved from her, she placed her hands on my shoulders.

"Gabriel, I love you. Thank you for making this night so special I'll never forget it." I pulled her in close, loving the smell of her, my nose sniffing her hair

"Fern, I love you to eternity and beyond. Never doubt that. Thank you for giving me your most precious gift, outside of your heart. I'll treasure both until my last breath."

Giving her a quick kiss, I lifted off the bed, reached over, and covered her with the quilt. Once in the bathroom, I throw the condom in the garbage and got a washcloth, wetting it with warm water, then went back to the bed. Fern's eyes watched me as I removed the cover and gently cleaned her, removing her virginal blood from her body. When finished, I tossed the cloth toward the bathroom and climbed into the bed, pulling her close to my body. We spooned until we both fell asleep in each other's arms. The first of many nights to come when we would fall asleep the exact same way.

As I sit in my chair in our home remembering that first time, I come to realize that Fern is my entire life. Nothing has happened since that night that we haven't shared, worked on, or gotten through together. Feeling like a part of me is missing, and it actually is because she's in a hospital across town, I realize how much of my entire world depends on her. For the first time since her diagnosis I feel true fear. Not knowing the outcome has me scared shitless because I know I can't live without her. She's every breath I take and every beat of my heart. And without her nothing else matters.

CHAPTER TEN

PRESENT ~ MAKING A STATEMENT ~

(Gabriel)

I must have fallen asleep because the first thing I hear is someone pounding on my door like the house is on fire. Trying to get my bearings, I push myself from the chair, heading toward the door. Opening it wide, a smile comes to my face. Yep, my calls have been answered. As Cadence, Trinity, Hope, Wolf, Axe, Jagger, Daisy, Willow, Archie, and finally Des and Dee Dee walk in, I feel a lightness in my chest that hasn't been there for a long time now. Not only am I dealing with Fern's illness but fighting my own weakness with those over-the-counter drugs and drinks. Each day is getting easier but there are still times I crave one or both of those pick-me-ups. Thank God I went in to see Dr. Jazbowski for help. The meds are helping me with the anxiety and also with getting some much-needed sleep. I'm finally starting to feel like my old self, with only the occasional tremors or shakes.

"Okay, Doc, what is it you need from us to make Fern feel better? We're up for anything, so get to explaining," Axe shouts out.

I look around the room and explain, "Can y'all wait a couple of minutes as we are waiting on a few more to arrive? Can I offer you something to drink while we wait?"

As I take orders, mostly for water or pop, I grab them out of the fridge, passing them out as the doorbell rings. Looking past everyone I manage to connect with Cadence's eyes as I lift mine then glance toward the door.

"Gotcha, Doc. Let me get that for you."

Bear, Stash, and Ugly come into the room, all looking like they rode cross-country.

"Shit, guys, my message said if this wasn't good time for you don't worry about it."

Ugly steps forward as their spokesman. "Doc, when it comes to you and your ole' lady there's nothin' we won't do. So what's your plan, but before that, I have to piss like a racehorse. Where's your can?"

Des lets out a growl. "Ugly, watch your trap. There are kids here."

As the biker makes it down the hall, we hear him mumbling, "Fuck, didn't know kids didn't piss. Must have been the horse comment..."

Des just shakes his head as the girls and Jagger laugh at Ugly's comment.

When everyone has something to drink and has sat down, I try to explain my idea.

"Not sure if anyone will be game, but Fern asked me to bring the clippers tonight so I can shave her hair. Chemo is making it fall out in clumps again so she wants it gone, not on her pillow each morning in handfuls."

Dee Dee lowers her head and I know she gets Fern's pain. For a woman, their hair is everything, so to lose it hurts deep. She raises her tear-filled eyes to me, her face looking sad as she shakes her head.

"So," I continue, "I came up with an idea and wanted to see what y'all think."

Later that evening as we approach Fern's room, I look back at the crowd, amazed at their dedication to my wife. Ugly, Stash, Bear, Axe, and Cadence are totally bald, just like me. We all have the same rags on our heads, thanks to Dee Dee. The girls: Archie, Willow, Daisy, and Dee Dee have each cut off six inches or more and are donating for wigs. Even Wolf took off a chunk of his hair to donate with the girls. I can't wait to see Fern's face when she sees the support we have from our family. As Ugly pushes to the front, directly behind me, he manages to hit everyone in his path with his bundle of balloons.

"You sure your ole' lady can't have flowers? Balloons seem more for a kid, ya know what I mean, Doc?"

"Ugly, she'll love them. I promise."

I open the door as Fern lifts her head from the e-reader on her lap. The look of utter shock, then the snort and laughter coming from my wife's lips is worth everything. I was right on with this crazy idea of mine.

"Oh my gosh, Gabriel! What have you done not only to yourself but to our friends?" She watches as everyone piles into the room, some staying in the doorway so as not to crowd her. Tears fill her eyes as she looks at the girls with their shorter hair, a question in her eyes.

Daisy pushes Willow forward. "Tell her, Willow. It was your idea to begin with." Willow goes to Fern, kneeling in front of her.

"We didn't want to shave our heads totally, not that we don't love you, Fern, but..."

Fern looks at the young woman touching her face. "Willow, I get it. I don't want to shave mine either. Just don't have a choice."

Willow continues on, "I read somewhere in a magazine here, while waiting for you the other day, about donating natural human hair for wigs for cancer patients. So we all decided that we would cut off at least six inches so we can donate to help someone who's going to lose their hair and would love a wig."

Fern grabs Willow off her knees and pulls her close as both women start to sob. I hear sniffles all around the emotion-filled room, that is until Ugly grabs one of his balloons and sucks some of the helium out. Looking around, he starts talking in a munchkin voice. Then everyone starts laughing as he starts singing, "I Am Woman, Hear Me Roar."

"For Christ's sake Ugly, Fern is sick enough, you don't need to make her want to toss her cookies. Whoever told you you could sing, dude?"

Everyone nods as Fern starts to giggle, then snort, then she loses it, totally laughing uncontrollably. Everyone joins in, which helps bring the mood back up which is exactly what Ugly wanted.

Fern looks around and then her eyes find mine. The look in her eyes fills my heart as she mouths, "Thank you, Gabriel. I love you." I nod and blow her a kiss.

Hours later it's just Fern, Cadence, Trinity, Baby Hope, Des, Dee Dee, and me. Fern is sitting in the chair clutching a towel around her neck, waiting for this to be over. As I approach her, she turns and pleads, "Gabriel, can you let Trinity do this for me, please?"

I understand immediately and hand the clippers to her. As I walk away, Trinity leans down to Fern, listening to her intently. As Fern continues to speak, Trinity shakes her head, hands shaking. Watching both of them, I see the moment it hits Trinity why she has the clippers in her hands. She starts to sob and Cadence grabs her as I reach for Baby Hope. In less than a moment Fern and Trinity are wrapped up in Cadence's arms as Hope is staring up at me, drooling on my shirt. After a moment, Trinity grabs the clippers again and glances at Fern. "Ready for me to give you the ultimate spa treatment?"

Fern's face brightens and she lets loose again with her laughter. "Give it your best shot, sweetie. I can't seem to do anything with my hair anyway."

As Trinity starts to remove my wife's hair, we connect as I watch her face closely but see nothing but pure joy there. I have accomplished my goal on this night, which could have been devastating to Fern, but this bunch of dysfunctional misfits that we call family have managed to make it nothing big.

When Trinity is done, Dee Dee moves toward them, reaching in her purse to pull out the bandanna she made for Fern. It is a tie-dye of bright colors and in the front is a beautiful picture of a small cabin in the woods surrounded by flowers. This is perfect as it is just what my wife loves the most, home sweet home. Amazing how something that could have been devastating turned into a group event with everyone laughing and enjoying each other's company.

CHAPTER ELEVEN

PRESENT ~ THE DAY HAS ARRIVED ~

(Gabriel)

These last couple of days have been so hard on Fern. I can tell she's feeling all the chemo and testing, and it's wearing her down. But today is the day we've been waiting for and she has been preparing for it.

As the daylight shifts through the blinds in our bedroom, I lie in our bed doing something I don't do often enough. Praying. I ask God to watch over my Fern and make sure that the transfer goes without any issues, and more importantly, that it takes and Fern can finally be free of her cancer and truly live her life. Reaching over, grabbing her pillow, I catch the faint smell of her unique scent. It eases my nerves. Pulling it close to my heart I take a minute to just be.

Getting out of bed, I do my usual morning routine, making the bed then hitting the bathroom and taking care of business. While I'm in the kitchen making coffee, I hear someone at the front door. Heading down the hall, looking through the small window in the door I smile to myself. Of course he would be here to make sure I'm okay. Opening the door I smile at Cadence.

"Whatcha doin' here, kid? Got nothin' better to do?"

As I move out of the doorway he enters, gaze on me, assessing where I am. I nod toward the kitchen. "Head that way, Cadence. I just put on a pot of coffee."

Shaking his head, he walks through the house and takes a seat at the kitchen table. "How're you doing, Doc? Can't fuckin' imagine what's going through your head. I would be fuckin' nuts, no doubt."

Grabbing two mugs, I fill them with the fresh coffee and sit across from him. I take a sip of coffee, trying to gather my thoughts, but before I start to say anything, he tells me his thoughts.

"No don't, Doc. There is no way that we wouldn't try to help both you and Fern, and I'm so grateful to Trinity for not only coming up with this but researching this shit for us. Got a good one, Doc, don't I?" Nodding my head slightly he continues on.

"Been thinking and I'm not the religious type, but I think God brought Hope to us for many reasons. One is he gave us a way to save Fern. Know it sounds crazy, but I don't think so. Trinity and I have talked about it. Too many things lined up for us to be here today, getting ready to do this. So all I have to say is I hope by the grace of God this transplant works and I'm fucking happy as a pig in shit that we're finally here. Only positive thoughts today, right, Doc?"

Grabbing his empty hand, I squeeze tightly as my throat locks up.

"Cadence, you know how Fern and I feel about you, but never will I be able to express how very grateful and thankful I'm to Trinity and you. Letting them use Hope's umbilical cord blood is such a gift and we'll honor all of you always. I haven't told anyone, not even Fern, but I'm scared shitless. So if you don't mind, can you stay by my side today? I would really appreciate it."

He returns my squeeze. "No other place I would want to be, Doc, no other place."

We sit quietly, each in our own thoughts, but linked together by our hands, saying a quiet prayer for the procedure to be a success.

As we get off the elevator, I think once again that the hospital staff probably can't wait until Fern's treatments are over. I see the waiting room is packed and everyone turns as Cadence and I enter. We greet everyone as we wait for word on what's going on.

Dr. Davids enters the room looking for me. Reaching over Cadence, we shake hands.

"Everything is ready. Wanted to take a couple of minutes to explain what exactly is going to happen. Today is day zero, as we call it. The transplant should take maybe one to two hours and looks a lot like a blood transfusion. Now once we are done, Fern will be put in a sterile environment and we will keep visitation to a minimum. Everyone can stand in the entryway, but she is very vulnerable between the chemotherapy and consolidation therapy, so her immune system won't be able to fight germs and she can't afford to get ill. You, of course, can go in but need to take precautions. Julie has gone over all the details with you already, so I just want to make sure you understand everything and have no questions."

Those closest to us are standing around me, giving me much-needed support so we all nod our heads and then Dr. Davids continues on.

"Remember the precautions once the transplant has taken place. We will be limiting the visitors allowed to see Fern. And those approved visitation will need to follow the strict guidelines, including sanitizing hands prior to entering. Also everyone visiting must wear a gown and mask before entering her sanitized room. No gifts enter without getting permission from Fern's nurse. No exceptions. I remind you of this again but wanted to make sure everyone understands how serious this is. For Fern it's between life and death.

"Doc, why don't you go and spend some time with your wife? We are getting everything ready but I can tell she's nervous. Calm her down, will you please? As for the rest of you, let's try to get a more comfortable place for everyone to wait until the transplant is done. Up on floor five, where the procedure is going to take place, is a huge waiting area."

I nod immediately, working my way through the crowd and go to my wife.

Entering her room quietly, I am shocked at how very fragile Fern looks. Between the treatments and radiation her skin looks grayish and her eyes have lost their sparkle. But even with all of this, she's still the most beautiful woman I've ever seen. Walking to her as she lies trembling under a mountain of covers, I sit on the edge of the bed. Just as I start to speak to her, two nurse's aides walk in with their arms full of blankets.

"Mrs. Murphy, we'll warm you up in no time. These here are warm blankets so let's switch them out."

Getting out of their way, I watch as they carefully remove the cool blankets, replacing them with the warm ones. Immediately Fern's eyes close and she releases a happy sigh. The girls leave and I take back my place next to her, feeling the heat coming off the blankets.

"Sugar, how you doing today? Dr. Davids explained everything and according to him the procedure will take just under two hours and then you will be in an isolation room, but I can still come in and be with you. I'll just have to take precautions." She reaches for my hand.

"Gabriel, I'm not worried at all. I've put it in God's hands. Need to say a couple of things to you so please listen, as we don't have a lot of time." Grasping my hand tighter, Fern struggles to sit up. I help her and lift the bed, adjusting her to make her more comfortable. Finally Fern glances at me then reaches for the bedside.

She grabs a piece of paper and holds it while looking at it.

"Gabriel, you have always been my knight in shining armor. Not like in the books I read, but as a real man who has never let me down. We have no idea what's going to happen but I need to get this off my chest. I love you and only you. If for some reason this doesn't work, I want you to put this in my file."

She hands me a DNR (do not resuscitate order). I start to panic.

"I hate to have to put this on you, but this is my wish. We will not draw this out if the transplant doesn't work. In the top drawer are other papers the nurses have helped me with. You are my medical power of attorney, but I also put down Cadence. Knowing you, Gabriel, not wanting to let go, you need someone who can have your back. Don't get upset, husband. I'm just making sure we have our ducks in a row and everything is in order. I will speak to Cadence in a moment, but you will listen to him if the time comes."

Taking in the determination in her face, I can only nod.

"Good. Glad we got that out of the way. Go grab Cadence because after I speak to him, I have a favor to ask you. Will you lie with me for the time we have left and hold me? I'm miss my husband's arms around me."

Getting up, I head out the door, telling Cadence that Fern wants to speak to him for a minute. As he walks past me, he leans in and whispers, "It's gonna be all right, Doc. I can feel it."

Just like the doctor explained, the transplant took over two hours. It's now a couple hours after that. By the time they completed the procedure and Fern went to recovery, then finally being moved to her isolation suite. There's a smaller room with a recliner that has a large glass so she can visit with those outside through the speaker. But right now she is lying in the bed looking out of it. Between everything she's been through physically and emotionally, she is at the end of her rope. As I move across the room, her eyes widen at me in the gown, mask, and booties. Her voice sounds scratchy.

"Gabriel, you look... um, well funny."

She actually giggles a bit, but then starts to cough as her throat is very dry. Immediately reaching for the ice chips the nurse left for her, I hand the cup to her as she starts to suck and chew on them. The relief in her face tells me she is in pain.

Sitting in the chair next to the bed, I grasp her hand under the blanket and whisper softly. "Sugar, I'm here now. Try and get some sleep. I won't let anything happen to you, honey."

Giving me a small smile, she does exactly what I said and in minutes she is out to the world. Watching her sleep, I feel the pressure ease a bit in my chest, but until we find out if the transplant has taken, my heart will continue to pound as my mind scatters all over. After a while, I rearrange the recliner so I am right next to her. I lean back, trying to get as comfortable as possible. Reaching over I twine our hands together. Even though my hand is covered by a glove, and our entwined hands are under the blankets, contentment fills me just by holding her hand. I say my nightly prayer before falling into an exhausted sleep. Day zero is finally over.

CHAPTER TWELVE

PRESENT ~ WAITING GAME ~

(Fern)

Gosh I didn't ever think I would be so bored, but this is ridiculous. Gabriel visits as much as he can, but between work and the remodeling at our house, he is looking exhausted. I told him to take the night off, stay home, and try to relax. Little did I know that without his presence I would slowly start to go insane. This is my sixteenth day in isolation. Everyone is super nice and the "family" all takes turns coming to the viewing area and visiting, still I'm so lonely. They all are trying so hard to make me laugh and fill my days, but nothing takes away the overwhelming fear that is slowly creeping its way throughout my body.

I'm not ready to die yet. Gabriel and I have too many things we want to do and see. We eventually want to try again for a baby. At the thought the most intense pain hits my heart. We have tried numerous times and each time I miscarried. None of the doctors or specialists could explain, but it became very apparent that I would not be able to carry our child to term.

So before this last diagnosis, we endured the procedure and harvested my eggs. After being fertilized the eight eggs are now frozen, waiting to be placed in a surrogate mommy. That thought makes me angry and sad at the same time. I feel like I failed not only both of us, but also our wedding vows, however, Gabriel has explained time and time again that it isn't my fault. He keeps telling me that anyone can make a baby but it takes a special woman to be a momma. Hearing him say those words always lets me know how very lucky I am to have him in my life.

Thinking about that, I reach for the pad of paper and pen. Since I have been in this isolation room, I have taken steps to make sure everything is in order in case this takes a turn for the worse. As hard as it is, each night I write a letter to each person who matters in my life. I started with the easy ones because even though I love everyone in the Horde, the relationship with the younger ones hasn't been through the test of time. So letters are in the top drawer for Daisy, Jagger, Willow, Archie, Axe, Prudence, and the bikers from the Asphalt Riders, Intruders, and Native Warrior Riders. Each club has been so supportive of both Gabriel and me that there were a couple of things I needed them to know. Especially those select few of the bikers who have been here from the start and helped with the charity ride—Stash, Bear, Ugly, and Enforcer. None of these letters are long, but just to let them know I appreciate and love each and every one of them. Letters to Wolf and Cadence were not that easy, as these young men are like my own boys even though they are men. Each of them is unique unto themselves, but have become important parts of mine and Gabriel's lives and if something happens, these men will have my husband's back. Looking at the blank stationery in my hands, I realize I have been putting this one letter off, as it is way too close to my heart.

Gabriel,

If you are reading this letter, it means I lost my fight. Please know you my lovely husband, best friend, and lover have made my life so much better just being part of it.

From the beginning to the very end you always were there for me.

Please, Gabriel, don't stop living, as that is not what I want for you.

Listen closely, my husband, I can't imagine how hard this is for you, but you are not alone. Let our 'family' help you through this time of grieving. It won't last forever.

I want you to hear me, Gabriel, no matter how much it hurts. Move on, love again, and find someone to share your life with.

You deserve all of that and so much more. Never feel guilty because you have done everything possible. Your devotion to me is what has kept me fighting to want to live. I do believe in the afterlife, and until we meet again, please know I will be watching over you, husband, always.

My world has been better because you were in it. My life was complete because you shared yours with me.

Finally, my husband, whom I have loved all my life and who until my last breath I was also totally in love with.

You completed me and for that I am thankful.

My final request is only this; be happy, Gabriel.

Please find your serenity and peace of mind knowing I will always be with you.

I love you, Gabriel.

Fern

Hoping with my entire being that my Gabriel never has to read this letter, I fold it and put it in an envelope, addressing it to him. Once I seal it, I place it with the others in the drawer, knowing I still have a couple to write. Tonight though, I am done as this last letter has torn my heart out, because just thinking of leaving Gabriel guts me. Praying that my body accepts Hope's stem cells and the transplant takes is my daily thought and prayer. There are no other options and as of yet my CBC counts haven't been greater than the required 500 for three days in a row. As the professionals keep telling us, we have to be patient as it takes time, especially with cord blood.

Just as I turn to try to get comfortable so I can sleep, the phone rings. Answering it with a soft, "Hello?" I hear the voice of the man who, despite the drama in our lives, can still make me tingle.

"Hey, sugar, didn't wake you, did I? Just wanted to take a minute and say goodnight before I hit the hay. How're you doing tonight?"

We share our day and night, and my pain lessens as I listen to the strong masculine cadence in his voice. It lures me to relax until I am almost asleep, holding the phone to my ear breathing heavily. Gabriel laughs.

"Sugar, go to sleep. I'll talk with you tomorrow. Love you, Fern."

I mumble half conscious, "Love you too, Gabriel." Then I place the receiver on the base before falling into a deep sleep as across town my husband does the exact same thing.

CHAPTER THIRTEEN

PRESENT ~ GOOD & BAD ~

(Gabriel)

Each day that has gone by without Fern reaching her consistent three-day goal greater than 500 ANC (Absolute Neutrophil Count) has started to weigh on her. Watching her trying to keep her spirits up is killing me because there's nothing I can do.

The only thing keeping her going is her new old friend. Lydia is also a transplant patient in the room next to my wife. They met by accident as Lydia's mom was bringing her children to see her through the visitor's window. Fern was visiting with Trinity, Hope, and Dee Dee through her glass and saw the little ones going by and calling for their mom. Of course it started a party between the people outside and the two women inside. Suddenly they realized they knew each other. After going back and forth, it came to them both at the same moment. St Francis Elementary School. They both went there. Small world. They reminisced about all the goofy things they did back then. Sharing similar traits like being quiet and shy, they were always together like peas in a pod. They unfortunately lost touch when Lydia met her then soon-to-be husband, who turned out to be abusive and a jerk. Both were ecstatic to find each other again.

That was about two weeks ago. Lydia and Fern have been spending as much time together as possible. They actually haven't been in a room together. That's too risky due to the transplants they both just received, but they have managed to communicate with their computers.

After meeting Lydia, I could tell she was worse off than Fern. It showed in her overall appearance. Fern has asked me to pick up a couple of things for her new friend since her mom, who was with Lydia's kids, is all she has. Fern shared that Lydia's mom is suffering from diabetes so it is taxing with the two young children both under five years old. Leave it to Fern from her hospital bed to arrange some free time for Ann, Lydia's mom, as Trinity—along with a reluctant Cadence—were planning on the kids spending the night with them and Hope.

"Sugar, explain to me why somehow you manage to make things better for everyone you know? Ann looked so relieved, just now ,leaving the kids with Trinity. Can't wait to see Cadence when he comes to get them."

Laughing I finish.

"That boy is in for a huge surprise as those kids are going to run his ass off tonight, no doubt."

Looking over to where Fern is watching all the action outside the glass, she shoots me a smile that causes her eyes to sparkle.

"It was the right thing to do, Gabriel. I'm blessed with such a huge support system while poor Lydia has no one, just her mom, Ann. I can't imagine being so alone and having two little ones on top of that. Did you get the stuff for the kids too?"

I nod my head in agreement. "Of course I did. New pj's for both, with two sets of clothes with new undies, socks, and gym shoes. Also each one will have a new stuffed animal to sleep with. And finally there were fleeces on sale so I got each of them one."

She turns and walks to me, putting her head on my chest, hugging me close. Now I have on a hospital gown and mask but still just her close sets my pulse racing. This is not remotely sexual but more emotional, something I desperately need. I pull her close and we stand together for a while just enjoying being close to each other.

"Fern, have you talked to Lydia about what she's going to do when she gets out of here? From what her mom says, her apartment is way too small and being a basement one, not suitable for her daughter and grandchildren to live in. I spoke to Ann at length and explained that Des and Dee Dee are trying to figure something out. Has Lydia said anything about the kids' dad?"

Fern just shrugs.

"Nothing about their dad except he is gone for good. She knows that the apartment isn't going to work but doesn't have any idea about what she is going to do. She can't maintain the three days, just like me, so for now we are both stuck here. I think she is avoiding even thinking that far in advance, Gabriel. It's just too much."

Just as she finishes, the door opens and Dr. Davids and Julie walk in, both in gowns and masks.

"Do you have a minute? We would like to talk to both of you," Dr. Davids asks.

"Well, I'm not going anywhere so I guess that means yes, come on in," Fern replies with a bit of a small smile gracing her face.

As we both sit on the edge of her bed, Dr. Davids and Julie step forward. That is when I notice the papers in Dr. Davids' hands. Catching his eyes, I see something in there that I haven't seen before. Hoping for some good news to come from him, I wait impatiently as they go through their usual protocol when they come into the room.

Checking all Fern's stats and seeing they are happy with them, Julie nods to him.

"Well, finally some good news, guys. Fern your ANC has been over 500 for the last three days. So after thirty-nine days we can consider this engraftment successful. Congratulations, Fern, we are now going to start to prepare you to reenter the world. It will take time and we need to be careful, but things are definitely looking good."

I turn to my wife and grab her, pulling her close. As my heart starts to beat rapidly and eyes fill with tears of happiness, I kiss my wife on the lips for the first time in over five weeks through my mask, looking in her eyes. Feeling her body start to shake, I pull her closer as she starts to sob uncontrollably from the emotional overload.

Continuing to hold Fern close to me, Dr. Davids explains that her body will be on overload for a while, and she will react like this sometimes. Julie comes to her other side, putting her hands on Fern's shoulders.

"Fern, come on now, try to relax. Let's not get too worked up, sweetie. This is a happy occasion but we still need to be careful. Try to take a couple of deep breaths and relax."

As we realize what this means, finally I see a light at the end of the tunnel. If everything goes the way Dr. Davids says it will, Fern should be home in the next couple of weeks, God willing.

Shit, I think I need to step up on the remodeling. Releasing Fern, I tell her that I need to speak to Cadence for a minute. As I leave the room, I turn and catch my breath. It has been so long since Fern looked truly happy and content. Her cheeks are blushed with color and her eyes shining, not sure if it's from her tears or just happiness. Winking at her, I head out to inform both Cadence and Trinity of the news. I also need Cadence to have the guys move up our deadlines because there is no way Fern is coming home and our house not being done. We have worked way too hard so far and though we're at the curve in the road and want it to be perfect, the remodel needs to be done perfectly when she comes home. Just like Fern is perfect to me.

CHAPTER FOURTEEN

PRESENT ~ KNOCKIN' ON DEATH'S DOOR ~

(Fern)

Opening my eyes, I feel like something is sitting on my chest and it is hard to breathe. Feeling like my nose is running, I go to wipe it and come away with snot and some blood. Knowing something is wrong, I turn and press the nurses' button waiting for them to come in, not daring to move. Eventually, an aide comes in.

"You need something, Fern? Oh my, are you okay, Fern?"

She looks me over and from the look in her eyes, something is definitely wrong, as the weight on my chest is getting heavier by the minute.

"Let me go get Julie, STAT." Starting to panic and being alone isn't helping me at all. I concentrate on breathing in and out shallowly through my mouth, trying to imagine a happier time. I close my eyes and see both Gabriel and me in our home last Christmas, the tree glittering with all the lights and all my decorations around the house. We were sitting in front of our little fireplace, holding hands, enjoying the holiday season. As my mind continues to see that scene, my body starts to relax which makes my breathing easier. The door opens with the clash of many footsteps but I hear Julie first.

"Fern, honey, open your eyes and tell me what's going on."

Doing as she asked, I am shocked at the crowd of people in the room, gowned and masked. Looking back at Julie, I try to speak but my throat feels like it is closing up. She immediately detects the problem, and leans over whispering in my ear. "Fern, sorry, close your eyes and go back to where you were relaxing. Don't worry, I will tell you everything we are doing. Just continue to relax and let us make you more comfortable."

Clearing my throat I say the only thing I can think, "Call Gabriel."

Knowing he's going to freak out, there is nothing I can do to prevent it. I need him here for many reasons, but mainly if something is going to take a turn, I have to see him one more time. The needle breaks my skin and the breath from Julie's whisper brushes against my ear.

"Fern, sorry. I should have warned you we are taking blood to check your counts. I'm not sure you need an X-ray, but I think you might have an infection or even pneumonia. We are also starting you on antibiotics, and once we know what it is will dispense some pain medication to make you comfortable. You're doing so well, Fern, hang in there. Okay?"

I just nod my head slightly, my eyes never opening.

I know the moment Gabriel walks into my room. The room feels like it is immediately filled with electricity. I can almost hear it humming. My hand is engulfed in his.

"Sugar, I'm here for you. I'm here now."

His voice sounds a bit off, but God only knows what he's walked into. Squeezing his hand to let him know I am okay; I feel him sit down next to me. As time goes by, I fall in and out of consciousness, as Gabriel never lets my hand go.

After all the tests, blood draws, and X-rays, Dr. Davids comes into the room to talk to us. Before he can get a word out Gabriel asks him, "Does this have something to do with the transplant? Is her body rejecting it or is it one of the hospital diseases patients catch when in here too long? Tell me, Doc, please. I'm going nuts here."

Dr. Davids looks at our hands, then at both of us.

"Gabriel, I understand your concerns but this is not rejection or anything remotely like that. This is an infection Fern has in her lungs that has progressed to a form of pneumonia. Now as bad as it sounds, we can manage this with some strong antibiotics and rest. For the mucositis we will be having Fern wash out her mouth every couple of hours and gargling with some salt water. Also we have some viscous lidocaine to give her some relief. As we fought this before, it's a side effect from the chemotherapy and radiation. It will take time, but eventually it will go away. I know it feels like you are swallowing glass every time you swallow anything, Fern. Definitely a setback, but nothing we can't handle. Fern, how are you feeling at the moment?"

Taking a minute to answer I try to speak, but my throat feels absolutely raw. Julie approaches the bed with a cup of something that looks like watered down jelly. She helps me lift my head slightly and puts the cup to my mouth. As I open, she helps me with the cup and as soon as the stuff hits my throat, I feel instant relief.

Oh my God, does that feel good. I try to swallow all of it, but she pulls the cup back. "Fern, take it slow. No rush. I'm not going to take it away. This will help with the swallowing and especially the pain."

Finally it's all gone and she lets my head back down. Looking to Gabriel I try so hard to smile, letting him know everything is okay, but I just don't have it in me. We were getting so close to being able to make the transition to the outpatient facility down the street from the transplant center. The next step to prepare my body for the final destination: home. I am feeling so depressed suddenly. This makes me think I will never get out of here, if it isn't one thing it is another.

As if reading my mind, Gabriel sits on the edge of the bed. "Sugar, don't let your mind run wild with those thoughts. This is just a step back that could happen to anyone. Remember what your body has been through and just try to take it easy."

I watch him as he leaves to get me something small and light to put in my stomach, my body weak, mind confused I lie back. The pressure is better in my chest due to the fact I am back on oxygen. Also they had me do a nebulizer treatment and added that to my regime. If I remember correctly, every four to six hours a treatment until my lungs are better.

I must have fallen asleep because Gabriel is gently shaking me awake. Slowly opening my eyes, the first thing they see are his stunning emerald-green eyes intently looking at me.

"Come on, sugar, I got you something to eat. We have some chicken soup and mashed potatoes. If you finish all of this, dessert is both Jell-O and ice cream. Let's get you sitting up. I'll put this pillow behind you and then lift the bed. Let me know when you want me to stop."

After he gets me situated and brings the side table to me, he starts to feed me the soup and a spoon here and there of the mashed potatoes the way I like them, drowning in butter. Giving him a quick smile between bites, I point to the hot tea. Watching him taking care of me, I think about how much I've put this man through. Not many men would stick around, especially when all they get is a sick wife and being alone all the time. Gabriel is a saint, no doubt. Never once has he complained about our situation and has supported me one hundred percent.

As he puts the cup of tea to my lips, I mouth, "I love you, husband." His smile warms my heart and soul.

He softly replies, "Right back at you, Sugar, always and forever, Fern."

He helps me finish my meal, including the ice cream, then helps me get comfortable. Looking around my room, noticing we are finally alone, he slips his shoes off, getting ready to lie down beside me.

Shaking my head I whisper to him, "Gabriel, no, I'm so sweaty and clammy. I would love a bath but that probably isn't going to happen tonight. Don't come into this bed as it also needs to be changed."

He immediately reaches for the nurses' button, pushing it a couple of times. As one of the aides comes in adjusting her mask, Gabriel glances at her.

"My wife's bed needs to be changed and please bring me some of those warm wet wipes for a quick sponge bath."

The aide is about to reply when he continues, "No worries, honey, I'm going to help her to the bathroom so she can use the facilities and rinse her mouth out with the lidocaine. Then will do a quick sponge with the wet wipes. Thanks so much."

As the young aide leaves on her mission from Gabriel, he goes into the portable closet pulling out a clean set of pj's. Holding up undies ,I shake my head no. I don't want them on tonight, as they sometimes are so restricting.

After my 'bath' and gargling I am exhausted but

still need to do another treatment with the nebulizer. When I finally lie back in my bed, I'm half asleep before my head hits the pillow. Feeling the bed shift, I know Gabriel is getting comfortable next to me. Pulling me close, my head on his chest, I let out a sigh. Something we all take for granted, but to be held in his arms feeling his heat penetrating and soothing my aching body. This is what makes me happy. As I start to doze off somewhere in the background I hear, "Sleep, Fern, best thing for you. Don't worry about anything because I'm not going anywhere. Dr. Davids even let me take off the mask so I can finally feel your soft skin."

Feeling his lips pressing on my forehead, I didn't realize until that moment how much I missed his touch. A simple kiss but to me it's my lifeline. Trying to get closer to him, I feel it first but then hear his laughter.

"Nothing ever changes, does it, sugar? Trying to steal all my heat, just like you do at home. Come on get closer and let's get some sleep. It's been a long day for you, get some rest."

The last thing before I fall into a deep sleep is his hand moving up and down on my back, stopping every once in a while to massage my neck. It brings a feeling of peace to my battered body.

CHAPTER FIFTEEN

PAST ~ PAINFUL MEMORIES ~

(Fern)

Reliving that horrible night when we lost our last baby is one of my worst nightmares. There are times when it all comes crashing down on me as I remember the events of that night. It still haunts me to this day.

I must have fallen into a very deep sleep and as my body tries to cope with the infection running through my weakened system, my mind goes back to another time when the pain overtook my entire body and soul.

Feeling a pain like never before, I doubled over, praying that it wasn't happening again. Reaching for my phone, I first dial 911 and then Gabriel. As another contraction hit, I knew what was happening. I was losing another baby. This pregnancy made it to the sixth month, which gave us time to fall in love with our child. My body was being torn apart and there was nothing they could do. My baby girl wasn't developed enough, as it was too early for her to be coming. I knew that. I'd been at the OB/GYN two days before and asked the question neither of us wanted to.

The doctor told us that if by some chance the baby came at that moment the survival rate was very low. Something about her lungs and how small she was. Yes, we were having a baby girl. As I heard the sirens, the pain ripped through my stomach as my mind started to grasp the darkness, realizing that once again I had let Gabriel down. They couldn't find a reason why my pregnancies wouldn't go to term.

I heard the front door open and bang against the wall as Gabriel came in screaming my name. Hearing the pain in his voice, I couldn't face him, so instead I let the darkness take me as my husband pulled me into his arms, holding me tight to his chest.

"Fern, sugar, it's okay. Don't leave me, honey. I can't live without you. No more. We're not going through this anymore. I can't stand to see you in this pain. Do you hear me, Fern? Come on, stay with me."

As he continued to rock back and forth with me in his arms, the sirens stopped right in front of our house. Knowing what would happen next, I relaxed into his arms and let go of all control, knowing that Gabriel would handle everything. I thought that as I lost consciousness.

As I struggled to come to, the first thing I saw was the soft yellow walls in a strange, large room. Hearing the beeps I knew I was hooked to machines, so trying to lift my head I glimpsed Gabriel in a chair next to the bed, holding my hand. I tried to squeeze his hand, but my body didn't seem to want to cooperate. I still somehow managed to get my fingers to move a tiny bit and tugged on his hand. Immediately he stood and came closer, his face inches from mine.

"Sugar, I'm here. I'm here."

Seeing the intense pain in those green eyes tore my already broken heart and I felt the overwhelming grief yet again. Another baby lost. I wasn't sure how many more times I could go through this without losing the final part of myself. Remembering my husband's words in our house, I knew the time had come to admit we couldn't have children. A heart-wrenching sob escaped from my parched lips as he grabbed my cheeks, looking directly in my eyes.

"Sugar, anyone can have a child but not many can be parents. We will adopt, foster, or whatever you want but we'll be parents. You were born to be a mom and I promised you that all your dreams would come true. It'll take some time to heal both physically and mentally and then we will start the next chapter in our love story."

Smiling, he leaned down and gave me one of the most passionate kisses I ever had. Feeling his unconditional love helped me chase away the tears. He was right as usual. We would survive this and find a way to go on. As long as we were together that was all that mattered to me.

Struggling to open my eyes, I hear Gabriel calling for me to open my eyes in the present as I am still in the past, recalling each miscarriage. My body goes back to each time, absorbing the pain as if it happened five minutes ago. My body feels like it is burning up as I struggle to push myself and open my eyes. Impatient hands grasp me like they are hanging on to me for dear life as my breathing becomes shallow and it actually hurts to take a deep breath.

Something is definitely wrong and I have no idea why I am reliving my past. My mind is playing games with me. My unconscious state drags me back. Maybe it's keeping me from experiencing the current pain.

Gabriel's voice strengthens me and I know I have to fight right now to get to him. I slightly open my eyes, seeing those phenomenal green eyes of his. Just feeling his presence isn't enough. I can't get there no matter how hard I try. I feel as though I am underwater and can't swim to the surface, but still continue to go down into the abyss.

Before I lose all my senses, the last thing I hear is Gabriel screaming and, I think, Dee Dee and Des trying to comfort him. Hearing my husband in so much pain rips at my heart but the dark is peaceful, comforting, and my body is so hot it feels blissful to have relief from all the pain running through my veins.

I promise myself that once I take a moment of relief, then I will fight to get to the surface, back to my

Gabriel. As the darkness calls me, I give in, my heart slowing as my breathing fades.

The deeper I go into that calm dark abyss, the more my body fails until there is nothing and the one machine goes silent and fades to a flat line.

CHAPTER SIXTEEN

PRESENT ~ TIC TOC ~

(Gabriel)

Hearing the call "Code Blue Room 231" didn't even seem real and I was standing right there. My beautiful wife Fern's heart stopped. Nothing. The flat line on that goddamn machine and I couldn't do anything for her but stand and watch. As more hospital staff run in with more machines, I can hear Dee Dee in the back crying uncontrollably as Des tries to quiet and comfort her. Me, I just stand here, hands to my mouth to prevent the screams from coming out. There was a god-awful noise coming from somewhere. Damn, shut it off whatever it is.

As the physician looks my way first then he looks at Des and says, "Get him out of here now, please." That's when I realize it's me making that god-awful noise. Dee Dee runs out of the room as Des grabs me, trying to pull me out.

"Fucking get your hands off me, Des, that's my wife

who might be dying or dead already. I ain't leaving. Get off me, asshole, now."

I can see the shock on his face because generally I don't swear, though since Fern has gotten sick my swearing has gotten worse, but it isn't every day the love of your life is dying in front of your eyes. Julie walks up to me immediately.

"Please, Doc, go right outside the door. I will be out as soon as I can."

Seeing the look of fear in her eyes, hope with some despair, I turn and walk out into the hallway.

I hear footsteps running down the hall and see Dee Dee's kids, Daisy and Jagger, coming right at me. Before I can do anything, they both fall into my arms. Daisy with tears on her cheeks and Jagger fighting to maintain control.

"Doc, we're here for you," is all I hear, as I am surrounded by teenage arms squeezing me tightly. That does it. I literally lose the strength in my legs and start to go down, and amazingly Jagger holds me up, leaning into the wall. Des comes around behind Daisy, grabbing on and not letting go. Not wanting to, I lift my tortured eyes to his and his are wet as he never loses eye contact with me.

"Don't fuckin' give up, Doc, on her. She's a fuckin' fighter and your love is the strongest I've ever seen. Stay strong, man, stay strong."

Des's words make me reach deep inside and pull myself together. Giving each kid a squeeze, we pull apart as I try to get my balance.

As we each take a spot on the wall, right outside of Fern's room, the waiting is the worst. More staff goes in and comes out but no one tells us anything. They have even pulled the curtain by the large viewing window. It seems like hours, but I know it is merely minutes, when I once again hear the sound of pounding feet. I don't know how I know, but in my heart I do, as I turn seeing the other man in Fern's life coming toward me, determination in his face as he reaches me, pulling me in tight.

"Doc, I'm here. Shit, got the call from Dee Dee; don't even know how I got here. Trinity is on her way. What's going on? Any news yet?"

Cadence spits out question after question, which lets me know he is panicking. Taking a deep breath, I pull away giving him a fist bump on the shoulder.

"Cadence, she coded about what ,Des, fifteen or twenty minutes ago? They pushed us out and we haven't heard anything since. That's all I got, kid."

Watching his face go white, I understand the ripping pain he is feeling in his chest. Fern is very special to Cadence. She helped save him and since then he has been there whenever she needed him. They have such a strong bond that knowing he can't do anything but wait is going to drive him insane.

Time stands still but at the same time feels like it's flying away from me. Being out here, away from Fern, is driving me crazy. As nuts as not knowing what is going on. Looking around once again, the hallway is filling up with Fern's *family*. As Cadence stated earlier, Trinity arrived here with Hope in her arms. Willow, Archie, and Prudence are sitting with Dee Dee's kids, trying to keep their attention on anything but what's going on in that room. Cadence's mom and brothers are here and it's nice to see all of them talking and supporting each other. That was a long time coming.

Feeling a presence, I turn to see both Wolf and Axe walking down the hall. As they approach, Wolf stops right in front of me. Reaching out he puts something in my hand. Looking down it's some form of a circle with four colors and some feathers.

"That is a medicine wheel which represents life and death, Gabriel. Each color is a direction with the center representing the heart. I give this to you now because you need it more than me. A wise woman gave that to me many years ago and it has guided me here and helped me survive. It is very powerful if you believe."

Listening to his calming voice explain this gift, I hold it carefully, thanking him for it. Axe also presses something in my hand. It looks like a doll of some sort but also an animal.

"That is a wolf totem. It's believed in our culture that if the wolf is your spirit animal you're very family oriented and mate for life. I wanted to bring something to you that reminded me of Fern and you, now hold it in your hands. Keep it close by Fern as her spirit animal will protect her when she needs it."

A calm peacefulness comes over me as I hold these two precious gifts. Cadence comes down the hall with a couple of chairs. As he pushes one toward me I collapse into it, elbows on my knees, hands holding my head. Not having the strength to even hold a conversation, I just wait to know if today is the day my heart and soul dies. I'm not sure how long I sit like that, but I feel the sudden change in the hall just as Cadence comes to my side, hand on my shoulder.

"Doc, Fern's physician is here."

Looking up I see Dr. Davids, Julie, and two other physicians waiting by her door. Getting up I brace myself, not knowing if I can handle what they have to tell me. *God, please don't take her from me. I'm not ready to let her go, we have so much to do and see.* These are my last thoughts as I approach the group waiting to give me their news.

Walking toward Fern's doctor from halfway down the hall, it seems like each step moves me farther away instead of closer. I can't get a read off of any of their faces. Poker faces for Christ's sake.

When I'm directly in front of Dr. Davids, knowing the Horde is behind me, surrounding me, supporting me no matter what, I glance at his face.

"Doctor, talk to me. What's going on? Is Fern...?"

I struggle as I say the next couple of words.

"Is Fern still alive?"

Clearing his throat, he looks behind me then at me. Finally I see a small smile.

"Yes, Gabriel, she is still alive. I'm not going to lie; it was close a couple of times. We lost her two more times before we were able to get her heart back into a normal rhythm. Right now she's barely conscious but her numbers are strong. She is still burning up with fever from the infection. Good news would be her body is fighting it off and the fever will break in the next couple of hours. Bad news is the infection has spread to her bloodstream and that would be disastrous with the transplant being so new. Right now all we can do is wait as the next twenty-four to forty-eight hours are critical."

He looks behind me.

"Why don't you all go home, as we want to keep visitors down to a minimum? Let's give Fern some time to rest and if she continues to improve then we can start letting visitors in, but right now I need to check on her. Doc, any questions? Come in when you are ready, but please put on the gown and mask. We want to take every precaution right now with everything going on. I'll be here most of the night, so if you need anything just have me paged, okay, Doc?"

Shaking his hand, which seems so small compared to what he has done for me. He saved my wife's life and all I got is a handshake. He must have seen the thoughts going across my face as he clutched my hand.

"Doc, all I did was my job. Fern is still here because of all these people supporting her. I truly believe not only in my medical ability but also in the power of family. Remember that always."

Shocked at his words, he turns and goes back in Fern's room as Julie steps up to me and, to my utmost surprise, gives me a quick hug. Glancing down as she looks up; her words will stay with me until I die.

"Gabriel, she fought for her life like a prizefighter. She would mouth your name when awake and each time she did her eyes got brighter and her color improved. Fern fought because she didn't want to leave you. The love you both share is awe-inspiring."

Releasing me, she also goes back into Fern's room. Turning to everyone, who have huge smiles on their faces, my gut tells me they aren't going anywhere. Wolf and Axe ask who is hungry and they start taking orders. Dee Dee goes to the nurses' station and comes back telling everyone that they can stay in the waiting room across and in the corner from Fern's room. As she finishes, two nurses come down bearing blankets and pillows in their arms. Seeing this, Axe asks them if they would like some food or coffee. They both ask for coffee. As everyone gets situated for a long night, I thank each and every one of them for their support and love.

Feeling blessed to have them in our lives, I finally head to Fern's room. I ask the nurse for a gown and mask. Putting them both on, I quietly enter the room. First thing I see are all the machines surrounding the bed she lies in. The noises are loud at first but slowly fade into the background. Walking to the bed, I am shocked at how small and flushed Fern appears. She seems to be resting comfortably as the nurses check her stats. Softly asking one of them what her temperature is I'm shocked to hear it's at 103.5. Holy shit, at what temp does it start frying your brain? They have cool towels on her even as she trembles. I reach for the one on her forehead and it's steamy hot. Taking it, wetting it in the sink with cool water, I place it back on her forehead. Gently touching her cheek, she feels like an inferno to me. I can see her taking shallow breaths each time her chest rises and falls. On closer inspection, she looks sickly and weak. There are tubes and IVs going in all over her. There isn't anywhere I can touch her. Turning and pulling the chair as close to the bed as possible, I hold her hand and pray. Because after seeing her, I know we are far from being out of the woods. Like Dr. Davids explained and now seeing it for myself the next twenty-four to forty-eight hours are critical.

Knowing this I try to get comfortable because I'm not going anywhere until Fern is out of the woods.

Closing my eyes for a moment I feel the beginning of a headache start. The pressure is like being in a vise. Part of this is left over from my stupidity months ago with the drinks and drugs I was using to stay on top of everything. Trying to relax, I run my fingers up and down Fern's hand. Suddenly feeling her fingers moving, I open my eyes to look directly into her beautiful hazel eyes. As she tries to focus, I see her lips saying my name over and over again. Finally in a hushed tone I hear the words that always make my heart full.

"Gabriel, I love you."

Those four words complete me. I clasp her hand to my heart.

"Sugar, you're my heart and soul. Always and forever, Fern. Until the day I die you will always have me. Baby, no words can explain how happy I am to see those beautiful eyes of yours and that awesome smile on your face."

We continue to hold hands and talk quietly until Fern finally falls into a deep sleep. Watching her, I feel my heart finally start to beat normally again. I look up and thank God for answering my prayers. Hearing the door open, I see Jagger and Cadence pushing in a recliner with a pillow and blanket on it. Somehow, they must know everything was pushed out of this room when Fern flatlined to make room for all of the doctors and nurses that worked on her. They both have on masks and gowns, stopping a distance away from the bed.

"Doc, thought you would be more comfortable on this. We took it from one of the waiting rooms. I had the nurses wash it down too, just to be cautious," Jagger says.

Shaking my head, I thank them both as they look down at Fern saying nothing. As they turn to go, Jagger turns back around.

"Doc, glad to know that all of our prayers worked.

Fern is like a second mom to both Daisy and me. I want a chance to tell her that."

He heads to the door and quietly under his breath tells me, "Love you both, Doc. Night." As the door closes behind them, I get comfortable in my stolen bed for the night and I smile for the first time today. Damn, I'm bone tired, but knowing my sugar is hanging in there is all I need to know. *We can face whatever tomorrow brings*, I think as sleep pulls me down.

CHAPTER SEVENTEEN

PRESENT ~ HANGING ON BY A THREAD ~

(Fern)

Sitting on the edge of the bed looking around, I think to myself, *another day and at least I'm still breathing.* Grabbing my tablet I FaceTime Lydia, who is in the room next to me. Because both of us are in the beginning stages of our transplants, we can't risk any infections. I hear the ringing but no answer. Wondering where she is, finally I see she accepted. Her face comes into view, and holy crap, she looks really bad.

"Hey, Fern. How you doing, doll face?"

Her breathing is ragged and coloring is off. Her eyes are dull and she is coughing a raspy, dry cough. Gosh, I have nothing to complain about, even though I still am burning up, just looking at my friend I know that I'm doing much better than she is.

"Hello, gorgeous. How's life treating you?" I reply back to her, not letting her hear how worried I am. Lydia is carrying a huge load with her cancer, two small children, and a diabetic mother. The stress alone could kill her, let alone everything else. As we both lie back on our beds, we catch up with each other. She tells me how concerned she was for me when Trinity explained how close I came. As she got choked up, I try to keep my emotions at bay.

Since the night I flatlined, I haven't been able to really let loose emotionally. Something is stopping me. I'm not sure if that is good or bad. I'm struggling to keep everything together.

In my own thoughts, I don't hear Lydia's question until she asks it again. "Hey, girlfriend, you listening, or are you in your own mind?" She lets a small laugh out and immediately starts to cough. Her lungs sound horrible.

"Sorry, Lydia, my mind drifted. What did you say?"

She smiles at me and gives me the hand as she reaches for an inhaler. Taking a couple of puffs, she turns back to the screen. "I was telling you how humbled I am by your family and all they are doing for my family. The kids had a blast last night at Cadence and Trinity's. All I heard about was how the kittens ran here and there, played with a ball, and slept with them in the spare bedroom. From what they told me, Cadence went all out. Haven't heard them so excited in a long time, so thanks so much, Fern. Mom got some much-needed rest. Oh, did you hear what Des is doing for Mom?"

Shaking my head, she continues excitedly, "Guess there is an old cabin behind Wheels and Hogs, right?

You were even thinking of moving there if you lost the house, Dee Dee told me. Well, anyway, they checked it out and it isn't as bad as Des thought at first so all the men are working on getting it livable. When Trinity went into the apartment Mom lives in, she was appalled. Between the dampness, darkness, and the mold, she told Cadence it wasn't fit for a rat, let alone the kids and Mom. Guess this is moving pretty quick too because Mom isn't doing too well with her diabetes. She's having some issues and the stress isn't helping. For the time being she is going to stay at Dee Dee's with her and the kids, and my babies are staying with Trinity and Cadence. How will I ever be able to pay you back, Fern, or all of these wonderful people?"

She finally takes a much-needed breath and her shoulders start to shake and she covers her face with her hands. Trying to get herself under control I softly say, "Lydia, take a minute and just let it out. I wish that I could walk into your room and give you a much-needed hug, but know that you have my support and we both will get through this."

As she tries to control her emotions, I keep telling her how strong she is and how lucky I am to have her next to me. Time goes by unnoticed as we both try to let go of all of our fears and worries. When we finally look at each other on our tablets with our blotchy faces, puffy eyes, and snotty noses, we both bust out laughing. It feels so good to just laugh, finally, when there is no more left in me and I am winded, I wipe my eyes and take a much-needed breath. Knowing I need to explain to her how the Horde works, I call her name softly.

"Lydia, this might not make sense, but when this group of people wants to help you, there is nothing you can do. It's actually something special to watch, as they don't accept just anyone. They will protect you with their lives and help in any way they can. The feeling of belonging is something so heartwarming, I have no words. Just know that from this moment on, you're not alone."

She reaches for the tablet, putting her hand on it as I do the same.

"Fern, thank you isn't enough, but know how humble this makes me feel. You're the sister I always wanted, but didn't have. From my heart, Fern, thanks for sharing your family."

It is time to lighten the mood, so I ask her about Charlie and Emma's night with Hope. Lydia's face appears brighter with each little story she retells of her kids. We laugh together, spending the morning giving each other support as we each struggle with the seclusion and loneliness being in isolation brings. As we gab, the nurses come and go checking our stats, IVs, and bringing in water and some crackers. Lydia yawns and tells me she is going to take a nap, so we say our goodbyes.

Putting my tablet down on the nightstand, I stand carefully, pulling the IV stand with me, going to the window to look outside. Each time I do this, it hits me hard how we as humans take so much for granted. Just looking out the window as people go about their normal days is something I treasure now, and others don't even realize how that little thing can change everything for a moment.

Fighting this infection has caused me to take some steps back and until the fever breaks, and the doctors know they have a handle on it, I am going to be stuck here in isolation. I can take the nausea, sores all over my body from the chemotherapy and radiation, being tired and emotionally numb from lack of human contact. But the not knowing is driving me insane, not to mention bringing on the depression. I can't let it beat me down, but it's a daily battle. I have been battling depression since the second miscarriage. It isn't daily, but when it hits, I go down hard. Gabriel can always tell when I am heading down that path, and together we can work hard to fight it back. I have seen counselors over the years and each one has tried to prescribe the newest drug. It's not that I don't want the help, but I don't want to be dependent on drugs for the rest of my life and being on those I wouldn't be able to get pregnant. Well, guess that didn't matter in the long run with my history.

My head is heavy now with all my thoughts and feelings. Weak from the fever and infection, I lie down in my bed, pull the covers up to my neck, and collapse into a fitful sleep.

CHAPTER EIGHTEEN

PRESENT ~ THE HORDE BUILDING A FUTURE ~

(Des)

Grabbing my cup of coffee, I get out of my truck slamming the door behind me. Fuck, I'm so Goddamn tired 'cause Ann had a really bad night, but I need to check on all of these projects we are all busting our asses on. Walking behind the Wheels & Hogs garage, onto the path that leads to the cabin behind the back parking lot, I see a lot of movement and action going on. Seeing Wolf coming out the front door, I walk toward him, giving him a smile.

"How's it coming, Wolf? Can you give me any idea or time frame 'cause we need to get this done as quickly as possible? Ann's place is a total disaster, according to Trinity, and with the kids, she is not thrilled staying with us and being separated from them. Not to mention she is having a rough go right now with her diabetes."

Walking toward the workbench, Wolf grabs a water, gulping half of it down immediately.

"Des, you will be surprised at how much we have been able to get done. Didn't know that Cadence had such mad remodeling skills. First off, as you can see, we put up new shingles because the roof was crap. Axe knows an HVAC company and they have worked with him to get the entire unit without breaking the bank, so to speak. They're going to be here later to install the furnace and central air. All the windows are being checked and replaced if necessary, but most seem to be in pretty good shape. Cadence has been working the last couple of days, after working in the garage, on the kitchen and main bathroom. We're lucky that when this cabin was built it was solid. Mainly it is cosmetic stuff we're doing. Gabriel talked to the lumberyard and got a real good deal on the hardwood floors because we're gonna put the exact same kind in both Gabriel's house and the cabin. Everything's coming together. Want to take a look inside?"

Nodding my head, I follow Wolf in through the new front door and let out a whistle. Damn, these guys are good. The kitchen looks awesome with lots of cabinet space, a new sink, and countertops. Now looking at them, I know they aren't top-of-the-line granite, but Formica. I don't think that will make a difference to Ann and eventually, Lydia. Walking through the house, noticing different things already replaced or fixed, I think to myself how good it's coming along. Stopping at the bathroom, I notice the new fixtures and one-piece tub surround. Good idea on that since we ain't got time for tile and shit. All the walls have been washed and there are cans of paint in the corner just waiting to be put on them. Dee Dee told me that they got Ann, Lydia, and the kids' favorite colors and that's what colors are going in the cabin. Walking to the staircase, I go up after telling Wolf where I'm going. The top floor holds all the bedrooms except one that is on the main floor. Gabriel decided Ann would be in that bedroom because of the neuropathy in her legs and feet. I walk through each room, noticing the floors have been sanded and are ready to be finished. Not only the master bathroom downstairs, but also this powder room has been updated. Leaning against the doorway between the two bedrooms I feel the pressure of everything on my shoulders.

God, when are we gonna get a fuckin' break? Knowing Doc is barely hanging on with all that's going on with Fern, but still managing to give a hand whenever he can, makes me think about what would happen if Fern doesn't pull through. Doc would be beyond devastated, and I don't have a clue what to do for him if that happens. Now we have taken on a small family, who have barely anything, and two very sick women with a couple of very young children.

Not trying to be an asshole, but looking at the total picture, we've got to figure out a way to help Ann and Lydia support their family. Too much shit's in my head and more keeps coming in. I thought the charity ride would solve so much and it did for Gabriel and Fern, but it isn't going to be enough to fix all we're trying to do.

Walking back down to the work area, I throw out my question.

"Okay, what's the plan for today? Dee Dee's at the garage so I have some hours to help out with today's job. What needs to be worked on?"

Some of the guys from town come into the cabin, as word has gotten out, Cadence looks my way.

"Hey, Des, got to get back to the garage and help Archie. She's drowning in maintenance work. Will be back after work."

Watching him leave as the men go upstairs, as today they are refinishing the hardwood floors finally. Not much else can be done once they start due to the fumes. Gabriel has already headed back to the garage, as he has a custom bike he's working on, which leaves Wolf and Axe to handle the work today. After making sure all is on schedule, I tell them I'll grab Dee Dee and go purchase the appliances needed for the cabin.

Walking to the back of my garage, I run my hands through my hair, knowing that this will again be a long-ass day with each of us busting our asses to stay on top of everything. I hope someday soon we'll get back to normal, or whatever the fuck that even is.

CHAPTER NINETEEN

PAST & PRESENT ~ STRUGGLING BETWEEN PAST AND PRESENT HOSPITAL STAYS ~

(Fern)

How did other women get through this, I think to myself? Another miscarriage and this one tore my heart out. I was almost five months pregnant and was just starting to show and feel those bubbles every pregnant woman talks about. Thank God Gabriel woke up as our bed was covered in blood. With all the blood loss and the ruptured ovary, the physicians told us I probably would have bled to death without my husband waking up, seeing what was happening, and calling 911 again.

Lying in my hospital bed, I finally realize that my dream of a huge family's never going to happen. Each time the loss is worse than the last. No, I don't mean that one pregnancy is more important. It's just that my body is failing and each miscarriage takes its toll on me both physically and emotionally. Been through each and every step, even going as far as to get the daily shots that are supposed to aid with a full-term pregnancy. Well, we see how well they work.

Clearing my throat and trying to battle the emotions down I try to act normal.

"Hey, Dee Dee, thanks for coming by."

My voice cracks as I speak and just know I'm going to break down. And that is exactly what I did as Dee Dee put the bag on the bed so I let her pull me close to her. It feels nice to know that someone other than Gabriel cares. But part of my problem is that I don't want to sit still. I always feel antsy, like I need to move after one of these losses, but have nowhere to go. We sit together as Dee Dee pulls a bag to me, showing me what is in it. Holy crap, it is a bag full of chocolate. Gosh, she knows me so well. As we quietly eat our chocolate, I can tell Dee Dee wants to speak, as her eyes are following my hand from the bag of goodies to my mouth and then back again but avoids my eye contact when I glance her way.

"Dee Dee, what's going on? Something you need to tell me?"

Shaking her head, she doesn't say anything for a minute, then replies back, shocking the hell out of me. "Have you ever thought of harvesting your eggs, Fern, and then doing in vitro fertilization and finding a surrogate to carry your guys' baby to term?"

My head jerks back so hard my neck cracks. Where's she going with this? "To be honest, in the past I did some research on that, but finding the right surrogate seemed to be pretty difficult. It would be so hard for me to have a stranger carrying Gabriel's and my child. I would feel like a third wheel. Don't think I can go through with that, Dee Dee."

She smiles weakly. "What would you do if I told you that if you truly wanted to have a baby, I'd be honored to carry your child?"

I look up to see my best friend with tears in her eyes.

"Fern, I'm petrified that one of these times you'll not get here quick enough and bleed out. If we do this, you'll be so close we can share everything with the pregnancy and you'll know already I wouldn't want to keep the baby. Just something to think about, okay?"

Nodding, I feel sleepy and close my eyes as Dee Dee takes a seat next to the bed, holding my hand as I doze off.

As I start to wake from the dream of my last miscarriage and Dee Dee's offer, I'm confused for a minute, trying to figure out why again I am in a hospital bed. My door opens and in walks my best friend. This time she is in a gown and has a mask on, but her eyes twinkle as she carries in a bag. As she makes her way to my bed, I have an intense feeling of déjà vu. Wow. My mind is playing tricks on me. Placing the bag on the bed, she sits next to me, holding my hand. "Fern, wait until you see all the work they've been doing at your house and the cabin. They're almost done, and dang, they both look amazing. Here, I took some pictures if you want to see."

Looking at her phone I tell her, "I would love to see the cabin, but don't want to see our house. Gabriel wants to surprise me with all the work they have done. I know they have put in all the top filtration systems and filters in the house for me, along with the new windows that let in the light without the heat. Forgot what he called it." As we catch up, I keep looking at the bag until Dee Dee pushes it my way laughing.

"Go ahead. You can look inside."

I knew it wasn't chocolate because I couldn't eat any right now as it makes me physically ill. Pulling the tissue paper out and glancing in, I can't believe my eyes. Reaching in I pull out some books and an Amazon gift card. Glancing through the books, I know Dee Dee knows my favorite authors, and they are all here. All new releases from Kristen Ashley, Kallypso Masters, and finally, Susan Fanetti. Looking at the gift card, I noticed that the amount written on the package is very generous.

"I know you're going out of your mind in here. Thought these would be able to get you out of your head for a bit. Also, the card is from all of us at the garage for your Kindle. Just trying to keep you on the road to recovery, honey, that's all."

As I usually am, whenever someone does something nice for me, I am overwhelmed with his or her generosity. "Thank you, Dee Dee. Please let everyone know how much I appreciate the gift card and the books."

As we spend some time catching up and I listen to what everyone is doing on my behalf, I kind of zone out, thinking I will never be able to pay them back. And that doesn't include what they are doing for Lydia and her family with the cabin. These folks are better than my own family, who I haven't spoken to in years.

"Hey, Fern, where did you go? You look upset. Come back to me, honey." Smiling at her I just shake my head as she continues giving me the scoop. As usual, when we are together, time flies and as Dee Dee looks at her watch, she jumps up and says, "Shoot, Fern, sorry. I've got to go get Daisy from school. Take care and let me know which of those books is the best because I want to read it. Always can use some recommendations, if you know what I mean." She finishes her goofy comment with red cheeks and a twinkle in her eye.

Crap, I wouldn't know as Gabriel and I haven't had sex in forever. Actually, I don't even think about it or want it anymore. Last thing on my mind. Just the thought of him seeing this emaciated body bruised and scarred doesn't spell sexy at all. Not to mention all the sores. Some are actually oozing with I have no idea what. Nope, no sex thoughts here.

Dee Dee gives me a hug and as she heads out, her mind is all over the place by the look on her face, I tell her, "Dee Dee, thanks so much, sweetie. Love you."

She turns her head and even though I can't see it

because of the mask, I know she smiles. "Back at you, Fern. Keep getting better. We have a lot more stuff to do together. Okay?"

Sitting on the edge of the bed, I reflect on Dee Dee's comments. I know she didn't mean anything by it. She didn't even catch what she said, but the innuendo regarding sex has me really tense. Gosh, how long has it been? Before I came to the hospital and probably months before that even? That was the last thing I ever gave any thought too. But what about Gabriel? How is he handling this dry spell? Crap, not a dry spell more like a drought, I giggle to myself.

CHAPTER TWENTY

PRESENT ~ TROUBLE KNOCKING ~

(Fern)

Waking up, I feel like someone is watching me. I look to the viewing window to see Katie—of all people—standing there, staring at me with the weirdest look in her eyes. I don't actually know her but have heard a lot about all the crap that she has done to both Des and Dee Dee since they got together. Also knowing about the scenes between her and my Gabriel makes me uncomfortable and angry. I struggle to get out of bed and walk to the area, taking a seat in an oversized chair.

Watching her pick up the phone to talk, I feel something akin to fear. Something is going to change as soon as she starts talking and I am actually afraid to hear what she has to say. But I don't let her see that and keep my face blank.

"Hey, Fern how're you feeling? Gabriel said the transplant took, as you finally got confirmation. Do you know when you'll be released?"

Watching her, she seems off a bit but I am trying to figure out why she's even here.

"Yes, Katie, we finally got the results that my numbers were consistent for the three-day period, indicating that the stem cell transplant took. If I may ask, why do you even care about my condition? This is actually the first time I have even spoken to you."

At my words, a wickedly devious look comes across her face as she smirks. "I was looking for a timeline, that's all, Fern. You know that with you in here someone has to take care of Gabriel, so I just want to make sure we are on the same page, if you know what I mean."

Feeling a pain like no other, I play dumb. "What do you mean *take care of my husband*, Katie? He's an adult and more than capable of taking care of himself. You're obviously biting at the bit and here to tell me something, so just spit it out. I don't feel like participating in this game you're playing."

I can tell she doesn't like what I said as she licks her lips. "Okay, Fern, you're right. I need to know when you'll be going home so I can clean my stuff out of your house and stop taking care of Gabriel's sexual needs. God, that man knows how to handle a woman, doesn't he, Fern? I haven't been so satisfied or so worn out in a long time. And that cock of his? So thick and long I can barely take all of him, but you know all of this already, don't you?"

Knowing that Katie is playing a dangerous game, I decide to play along for a bit to see where she is going with this. Gabriel told me everything and I would believe him over this slut any day. Watching her reaction as she spews her lies, I realize suddenly how desperate she actually is. Putting two and two together, I finally understand. She's doing this because of Des and Dee Dee. More so Des as she keeps mistakenly mentioning Des instead of Gabriel and doesn't even know her mistake. When she finishes I look at her. "Katie, I think you've said enough. It's time for you to go. Let's not make this worse than it already is."

She smirks at me. "Fern, you are so naïve if you think that Gabriel is waiting for you to come home. He's too much of a man for that." I lift the nurse call button and press it. She turns abruptly and leaves.

As I wait for the nurse, my mind goes over what Katie shared with me. I know that Gabriel hasn't seen her since the last time because he would have told me. Trying to think of a reason for her to be so cruel to me, especially at this time when I don't even know her, it finally occurs to me. She knows Dee Dee and I are best friends. She's hoping that I tell Dee Dee what she said so then my friend will confront her about her BS story. *Well, sorry to disappoint you, Katie, but not telling Dee Dee anything,* I think to myself as the nurse comes into my room.

CHAPTER TWENTY-ONE

PRESENT ~ SOMETIMES LIFE DEALS YOU A DEVASTATING BLOW ~

(Gabriel)

Watching as nurse after nurse goes into Lydia's room, I know something is going on. I'm sitting next to Fern's bed as she takes a much-needed nap. Just as I am about to get up and see what is happening, a "Code Blue to Room 233" is called on the intercom. Fuck!

Carefully removing my hand from Fern's, I make my way out of her room and go next door to Lydia's. Not entering, but standing close to the door, I can hear some of what is going on. It doesn't sound good at all. Hearing the nurses and doctors going through the same procedures they did when Fern flatlined, I step back and wait to see what happens. Glancing down the hall, I see Ann and the two kids coming this way. Knowing they have no idea what's going on, I rush down toward them. Ann looks up and must read my face as she pulls both kids to her and stops. Watching me, she seems to grasp that things are taking a turn for the worse. When

I reach her, I grab Emma up in my arms. "Hey, guys, let's go to the waiting area. There are nurses in checking on your momma. Okay?

Ann grabs little Charlie's hand as we turn and head to the waiting area. Both kids have backpacks so they sit at a kids' table and pull out some coloring books with crayons. As we sit down on a love seat, Ann finally asks, "Gabriel, what is going on? You're really pale. Oh God, is it Lydia? Or is something going on with Fern again?"

Trying to stay calm, I give her a small smile. "No, Ann, it isn't Fern this time. Something was going on with Lydia that I am sure you don't want the kids to see. Thought we could just sit in here for a while until they get everything under control." Grabbing her hand, I give it a squeeze and we just sit quietly watching the kids.

Finally unable to wait any longer, Ann stands and looks down at me. "Gabriel, can you keep an eye on those two? I need to see what's going on. The waiting is driving me crazy." I nod as she leaves the room. Watching those two precious babies, I wonder why this shit keeps happening to the good, nice people. Fern and Lydia are two special women, who always put others before themselves, and here they both are fighting for their lives. Watching as Charlie helps his little sister with her coloring, I pray that everything works out for these two. *They already don't have a daddy;* I think to myself.

Suddenly, I hear a loud wail followed by uncontrollable crying. The kids look my way as Trinity enters the room with Hope in a baby stroller. She quickly makes her way to me. "Doc, I'll watch the kids. Ann is losing it down the hall. Go make sure she is okay."

I get up and as I enter the hallway, something in my gut tells me there's nothing I can do for Ann. Watching the doctors and nurses around her, Ann's shaking her head while her body is racked with violent tremors as tears fall down her face. When she finally sees me walking toward her, she stumbles my way, falling in my arms. Trying to console her, not knowing what's going on, I glance at the nurses and they only shake their heads. Feeling the agony coming off of Ann, I quietly ask her, "What is going on? Has Lydia's infection gotten worse or is it something to do with the transplant? Please tell me what's going on so I can help."

She raises her head to look at me. "Nothing you can do now, Gabriel, we lost her. Lydia is dead."

Feeling like she punched me in the gut and not knowing what to say, I just hold Ann close as she lets her pain out through her tears. "What am I going to do with her babies? How am I to explain that they will never see their momma again? Oh my God, Gabriel, how am I able to take care of Charlie and Emma as I can barely take care of myself? Oh God, why did you take her? Why didn't you take me instead?"

Feeling hands on my back, I turn to see Dee Dee standing there. She motions for me to hand off Ann and I do after giving her one last squeeze. Pulling back, I lean against the wall, watching Dee Dee walk Ann the opposite way of the waiting area to a room Lydia's doctor is waiting at. As they enter, Dee Dee turns to me and gives me a very sad look, then follows Ann in to speak to the doctors about what went wrong for Lydia.

Knowing I need to let Trinity know what's going on, I head toward them when it hits me. Fern is going to need to be told, as she and Lydia were pretty tight since they spent so many hours on that face stuff. We had even talked about making sure when they both were released that we helped Lydia out with not only the kids, but also with Ann. Holy shit, this is going to devastate Fern. She'll be gutted.

Damn it. Why doesn't anything ever work out right? How in one day did Lydia get so bad that they couldn't save her? My mind is all over the place as I approach Trinity. She has Hope in her carrier while she is coloring with both of Lydia's babies. She looks up, sees my face, and immediately puts her hand to her mouth. Watching as she tries to hold it together, I just nod and motion for her to come to me.

She says something to the kids, then reaches down touching her daughter's cheek for a minute. Then she walks to me, watching me with her eyes. Once she's directly in front of me, she asks, "What happened, Doc. Is it Fern? Please tell me it isn't Fern."

Glancing behind her at the kids, I look back at her. "No, Trinity, it isn't Fern. It is Lydia. She just passed away."

She gasps and immediately looks back at the kids

then to me. "Oh, no. Please, no. What about those babies? Who's going to take care of them? Ann can't. Why did this have to happen to such a nice person? Doc, why?"

As we look at each, other neither of us has the answers to that question, but suddenly I realize I need to get to Fern and be the one to tell her she lost her good friend.

After putting on the gown and mask, I enter Fern's room. She turns toward me and I can see in her face that she knows something is going on but isn't sure what that something is. She looks as though she has put two and two together. Feeling like my heart is going to fall out of my chest, I make my way slowly to her bed, grabbing her hands in mine, kneeling in front of her.

"Gabriel, what's going on? All I keep seeing are doctors and nurses going by and then I heard an awful sound. I couldn't make it out. I've been trying to FaceTime Lydia, but she isn't answering. Tell me, Gabriel, please. Something didn't happen to her, did it?"

Squeezing her hands, I move my hands to hold her face in them. Taking in a breath, I gaze into my wife's eyes. "Fern, I don't know how to say this, so I'm just going to get it out. Just remember, I am always here for you. Fern..." I take a breath, mumbling, "son of a bitch" to myself. "Sugar, I'm so sorry, but Lydia passed away."

Immediately she pulls away from me as a keening sound comes out of her that sounds like she is in unbelievable pain. She tries to get out of bed, but is too weak, so she lies back, her fists punching the bed underneath her. Ignoring me, she reaches for the iPad and hits the button to do that FaceTime, but Lydia doesn't answer.

Fern's struggling for breath and is overcome with intense grief. I hit the nurses' button as she turns and actually growls at me.

'Why are you calling the nurses' station, Gabriel? Are they going to be able to bring Lydia back? If not, I don't want them in here by me with their pitying looks."

She looks around the room, shaking as she sobs loudly. Suddenly she's gasping for air and I reach for the inhaler, trying to give it to her as she repeatedly pushes my hand away and continues to choke.

I feel totally helpless as Fern has one of the worst anxiety attacks I've ever seen her have. As the nurses enter the room, they take one look at her and immediately jump in to assist her in this time of need. One nurse puts the oxygen back on her face as the other gets the nebulizer together, giving it to Fern to put into her mouth and breathe in and out. Her eyes never leave mine as she takes the treatment. Then, when she finishes, Fern lies back on the bed. Looking around her room as if she hasn't seen it before, she struggles to get herself together. Knowing she's about to have a breakdown, I pray that we can control this, as she isn't fully recovered from the pneumonia yet.

Julie walks in and takes a quick glance at us, then goes to the medicine drawer to take out a syringe. "Honey, I'm so sorry. This will help you to calm down some."

Fern shakes her head. "I don't want to calm down, Julie. I want to know what happened to my friend, who I spoke to just this morning. Why couldn't you save her? Who's going to take care of her kids or watch over her mom? God, those poor babies won't ever know how special their momma really was."

Finally realizing she's at the end of her control, I go around the bed, reaching for Fern's hands. She watches me but does nothing as I gently take her hands into mine, rubbing my fingers over the tops of hers. Watching her watch me unnerves me with that strange look in her eyes.

"Fern, don't even go there. We should be consoling each other on the loss of such a phenomenal woman, not fighting each other. We need to honor Lydia and be there for Ann, Charlie, and Lil' Emma. Come on, sugar, you have it in you, I know it."

Feeling like I'm not getting through to her, I pull her to me, holding her close. I feel instantly when she lets go and the sounds coming from her nearly kill me. I have no idea what to do to make this better. Fuck, there are no words to make losing a friend better. Especially when you and that friend shared a disease that could kill you at any time. I can only imagine what's going through Fern's mind at this moment. Rocking with her in my arms, I try to console her.

"Sugar, we'll get through this. I'm so sorry, sweetie. She was a wonderful woman who didn't deserve to die. Come on, sugar, don't work yourself up. We need you to be strong. Let Julie give you something to help you. Please, Fern, for God's sake, I can't have anything happen to you. I wouldn't survive."

Fern's head jerks up as she gazes into my eyes, hers filled with tears. "Okay, Gabriel, you're right. Julie, please I'm so very sorry for being mean to you before. I know both of you only have my best interest at heart. I'll take the shot as long as I don't fall asleep. I want to be awake when Ann gets here. I need to be coherent and functioning."

Leaning toward me, she places a soft kiss on my lips, then lies back down waiting for Julie to give her the shot.

"Gabriel, we're going to have to help Ann through this. Lydia told me the other day her mom's diabetes was getting worse every day. Ann has finally gone to see an endocrinologist and they are working on getting her on the right medication. Lydia was thrilled that finally her mom might start to feel better and thanked us for introducing them to Trinity. Oh, Gabriel, what's going to happen to Charlie and Lil' Emma? Who's going to raise them into the people Lydia wanted them to be?" Shaking with her emotions, all I can do is pull Fern to me and console her.

CHAPTER TWENTY-TWO

PRESENT ~ NO ONE SAID LIFE IS FAIR ~

(Trinity)

Sitting in the waiting area, watching the kids, my heart's breaking for Charlie and Emma. Crap, my mind can't even comprehend what's going to happen to them. Ann is a wonderful grandma but she's in a bad way right now with her health. That's why the guys are busting their humps to get the cabin ready for all of Lydia's family. Wiping tears from my cheeks, I realize Lydia will never see all that was done for her. Hearing a commotion in the hall, I raise my eyes as Ann comes into the room, her gaze frantic until she sees the two little ones at the table playing and coloring. Her face shows total devastation as she catches me watching her, and as I rise she comes right to me, falling in my arms. "Ann, I'm so very sorry. We're here for you and the kids always." As she tries to gather herself in front of her grandkids, I can feel the effort is wasted. Ann is emotionally done and I'm worried as she is having issues with her diabetes and stress is known to affect the disease.

Holding her close, I feel the change in the room immediately. Raising my eyes to the doorway I see Cadence, Des, Dee Dee, and Daisy coming my way. Dee Dee nods at me as she gently pulls Ann to her, taking her to a table along the far wall, away from the inquisitive eyes of Charlie and Emma. Cadence goes directly to the children, getting their attention, and starts playing some game with them. Des walks to me giving me a kiss on the cheek. "Never ends does it, Trinity? Can't understand why this fuckin' happens to the good folks while the assholes live a long healthy life for Christ's sake. She was such a nice lady who had shit luck. Have you had a chance to speak to Ann regarding what she plans to do? I know they don't have a lot of money so Dee Dee and I talked. We can help her with a funeral if she wants to go that route." My heart fills even more and I realize that in a short time I have come to love Des as a father figure, even though he's not that old. He can be dominating, alpha, and a bit of a pain in the butt but his heart is pure. "Des, she hasn't said anything, just grabbed on to me and hung on. I think she is in shock."

We both look toward the two women who are sitting at a table in the far corner. Dee Dee is nodding her head as Ann speaks to her. "Do you know what happened that she took such a turn for the worse? Last I heard was that both Lydia and Fern were doing better. Fuck, how's Fern? Is Gabriel with her? God damn, this is not what she needs with everything else going on." My head is spinning with all of his questions.

"Take a breath, Des, I can't keep up with all of your questions. Gosh, how does Dee Dee do it? I have no answers and now I have the beginning of a headache. Maybe we should go sit with them and see what Ann is saying and that might answer some of your questions, Des." He looks down at me with a shit-eating grin on his face. "Okay, Trinity, sorry, sometimes I get ahead of myself, and as Dee Dee always tells me to *count to twenty and take a breath* as that gives her a chance to catch up. Guess you women just can't grasp all that's me, huh?"

Giving me his heart-stopping, panty-dropping smile, he grabs my arm and we walk over to the table. As we approach, I hear Ann ask Dee Dee, "What am I going to do with Lydia's babies, Dee? My endocrinologist just told me that they're thinking about putting me on an insulin pump because my body is starting to shut down. Those little ones deserve so much more and now they don't even have a momma. I don't have the means or energy to do this. Why did God take my daughter when he should have taken me?" Her head in her hands, Ann starts to cry quietly as we all try to console her.

Des being Des, he starts to take control of the situation by talking to Ann. "Ann, you know I would do anything for you and those children. Lydia and you are part of the Horde so we're gonna be here for you, no matter what. Is there someone we need to call for you? This is going to be one of the hardest things you have ever done, but we're gonna have to talk about what you want to do with Lydia. Do you know her wishes or do you have any idea of how we should proceed?" As Ann starts to talk, I watch her and realize how lucky in my life I have been. Besides my mom, I've never really lost someone close to me who matters. Now with Cadence and Hope in my life, I have finally come to realize how much Doc has to lose if Fern were to take a turn for the worse. Thinking on this, I immediately rise, while Des continues to question Ann, and tell Dee Dee I'll be right back.

Going down the hall, I put on the gown and mask required to enter Fern's room. Knocking softly, I push the door open to find her in Gabriel's arms sobbing uncontrollably. Looking at his face the intense pain in his eyes nearly drops me to my knees, but I know what I have to do. Moving forward slowly, as not to startle Fern, I stop in front of them and crouch down. Taking her hands from Doc, I squeeze them until I have her attention. As she glances at me with her eyes full of tears, I softly lean forward and bring my mouth to her ear, "I'm here for you, Fern. Always will be as you were there for me when I needed you. I know you're hurting as you have just lost your friend but know that Cadence, Hope, and I are always going to be here for you. We love you and need you in our lives." As she starts to calm down, something tells me that this is the time to give her what I have wanted to for a while now as she is such a phenomenal woman and has been in my corner from the start. "Fern, look at me please." Her head rises up. "There's something I've been wanting to do for a while now and just haven't felt right, but now is the time. Lydia's passing shows me that life's way too short to wait for the perfect time. I want you to know I love you with all my heart and consider you the mother I never had." Hearing her gasp, as Fern's eyes get huge I tell her what's in my heart. "Love you, Mom. I'm sorry you lost your friend. We will get through this together as a family."

(Gabriel)

The last couple of days have been crazy. As I sit on Fern's and my patio looking out at the moon and stars, I think back to that moment in Fern's room when Trinity called her Mom and told her she loved her. At that moment nothing, and I mean nothing, could have been said that would have helped Fern as much as those eighteen words. Immediately my wife seemed to rise from within and took control of her emotions. She pulled Trinity to her whispering in her ear. I didn't want to intrude on their moment so I gave Fern a kiss, told her I would be back, and went to check on Lydia's children. Finding them with Cadence, Wolf, and Willow playing in the waiting area, something told me everything would be all right eventually. Watching Dee Dee and Des with Ann, that was who my heart went out too. The kids were young and wouldn't understand fully what they lost but Ann would.

Putting the beer bottle to my lips I silently and guiltily thank God for sparing Fern. Yesterday, we buried Lydia in the small cemetery in town with the entire Horde in attendance and some of her nurses too. Broke my heart to see Charlie and Lil' Emma with Ann watching the coffin being lowered into the ground. When Charlie reached for his sister's hand to pull her close to him, I just about lost it. Thank God we found each other because to imagine Ann going through this by herself is unthinkable.

I spent last night with Fern as she was shredded that she couldn't attend the services. Dr. Davids explained that it was too soon since her last infection to chance it, but that didn't help her deal with this at all. We finally had the conversation about if it could happen to Lydia then it could happen to her also. After getting Julie to explain that Lydia's body had not been able to recover from the intense chemotherapy and radiation that was necessary for her bone marrow transplant and that was essentially what killed her. The infection was just the final straw. Trinity came up with the idea and had asked Ann first before giving Fern the option. At the church and the funeral Trinity took Lydia's iPad and had Face Timed Fern so she was present at her friend's funeral. Ann went as far as to have her say a couple of words. Fern panicked and was worried, but as always, she did beautifully. Softly spoken and humbled, Fern introduced Lydia to everyone there and explained to him or her the love of a mother for her children. Fern shared some of the conversations that she and Lydia had and their concerns regarding their cancer and what would happen if they didn't survive. Finally Fern read a poem that Lydia shared with her that had everyone in tears. It went something like this:

I pray each and every day to be able to treasure my children and their ways

But something tells me that my days on this earth are limited and my time with them will soon come to an end

So I value each minute I spend with my children, telling them often how much Mommy loves them

Because when I am gone, I want them to know that they were loved, wanted, and needed

As life takes them down a different road to a new journey

While I pray that their lives will be filled with love, security, and peace

As my plans for them come to play as their new family helps them move forward from my passing

All I can do is hope and pray that they share with Charlie and Emma how much their first momma truly loved them, every minute of every day.

'Til we meet again, my beautiful children, know my heart beats because of you.

. . .

Trinity made sure that Fern was connected throughout the entire funeral. At the cemetery when everyone was given a different color Gerber daisy, Trinity took to explaining to Fern, "Mom, the bright yellow one is from you to Lydia as you were each other's sunshine." My heart was in my throat watching her toss that flower on top of the casket, holding the iPad so my wife could watch and be part of her friend's funeral. At that moment I couldn't love Trinity any more than I already did. She is the reason Fern is still here and why we have a future to look forward to. With all that she has been through in her young life, it didn't ruin her soul. *Trinity and Cadence are the children of our hearts* is my next thought.

Tonight, after eating dinner with Fern who then insisted, I leave and go home to get some much-needed rest, I totally agreed with her request. These last couple of months have been physically and emotionally draining on me. Not to mention my problem with the energy drinks and over-the-counter pills. I'm finally feeling like myself, even though I seem to tire more easily. And still at times crave that shit.

Feeling a bit lonely but more alone is strange for me. In all the years Fern and I were married I never felt alone, but tonight for some reason I'm fighting that feeling. Maybe it's the loss of Lydia, which is way too close to home. Not that I wanted to think about it, but if something were to happen to Fern my life would never be the same. She is everything. Hearing the doorbell I swear under my breath. Come on, can't I have just one night?

Going back in the house to the front door, I smile to myself as I open the door to Trinity, Hope, and Cadence. In Cadence's hands is a huge bag from Dairy Queen, which they all know is my favorite. "Per our orders from Fern, we're here bearing treats. Inside is an ice cream cake from your favorite place so you gonna let us in or do we get to eat this shit all by ourselves?" Cadence asks with a smirk on his face. Pushing the door open so they can enter, I reach over and grab Baby Hope from Trinity as she walks by. The baby girl lets out what I think is a giggle as I blow a raspberry on her little belly. Heading to the remodeled kitchen, the feeling of being alone leaves instantly as I watch my family making themselves at home, while Hope puts her small hand on my heart as she continues to giggle as I tickle her. As usual, Fern knows exactly what I need.

CHAPTER TWENTY-THREE

PRESENT ~ LIFE GOES ON ~

(Gabriel)

As we watch Dr. Davids enter the room, Fern and I are on eggshells. Today we find out if she can be released to the outpatient facility a couple of blocks from the hospital. This would be the next step to getting her home. She has been in the hospital for, I think, four months and she's ready to get out. It has been almost a month since we lost Lydia. Ann has had some rough days and even ended up in this hospital when her sugars were out of control. Cadence and Trinity have taken on the responsibility of Charlie and Emma, along with the rest of the Horde. Ann stopped by earlier, telling us that an attorney had contacted her about Lydia's will. It has taken his firm a while to find Ann as she had moved from her apartment to the cabin behind the garage and had not changed her address yet. She told me that the will was going to be read next week and that they were going to call me with the details, as they requested both Fern and I to be present. Well, not sure Fern will be present, but I definitely plan on attending.

Dr. Davids approaches us with a blank look on his face. Damn, the man could have been a pro at poker. Looking at the papers in his hands he says, "Well, guess I better give you my decision as you both look like you are ready to pass out. Fern, you have recovered nicely from the infection and I see no reason why you can't take the next step. I'm suggesting you go to the outpatient facility for the next two to three weeks to acclimate yourself to living outside the hospital and prepare you for your final step, which is going back home."

I let out a huge "Whoopee," grabbing Fern around the waist and planting a kiss on her lips. Her hands land on my shoulders, and I feel her fingers digging into my skin so I pull back, thinking I am hurting her. But there is only a beautiful expression on her face.

"Gabriel, we're one step closer to having our lives back. I'm so happy, aren't you?"

Giving her a soft squeeze, I just shake my head. The smile on my face says everything, but I can't speak as choked up as I am. Dr. Davids waits until we give him our full attention.

"This is a very scary step for you, Fern. We understand how hard it will be for you when you start to get back to living your life. Do you have any questions for me? Julie will be in later to go over all the restrictions and what could be harmful to you."

I look from Dr. Davids to Fern to see her blushing, her cheeks a pretty pink.

"Sugar, what's the matter? If you have questions you have to ask him, so you know what's going on and how to prepare."

Shaking her head, Fern struggles on, "Dr. Davids, my body has really changed and I am wondering will the feeling of being outside of my own body ever go away? Also, I have noticed that at times I get really angry or have no patience and that is something new."

Fern clears her throat, glancing at me quickly before she returns her attention to the doctor. "Will I ever get the feeling back to be umm, you know... be intimate with Gabriel again?"

We both watch Dr. Davids as he moves to the little sitting area, motioning us both to take a seat. Fern twists her hands in her lap, so I reach over and grab them, just to keep her hands still.

"Fern, you and your body have been through hell, best way to describe it. The chemotherapy and radiation alone have altered your body. The loss of all of your hair, fatigue, and the mucositis in your mouth are just a few physical signs you are suffering with. Thank you for telling me about the anger issues because the steroids cause that, and we call it *roid rage*. We'll keep an eye on that and start to wean you off of the steroids. For the feeling of being down, we can prescribe some anti-depressants. Now, for the intimacy, we spoke about this prior to the transplant. This is one area I don't have an answer for you because everyone is so different. Some women lose all of their drive and never want to have sex again. Some become extremely dry in the vaginal area and have to use some lubricant every time they have intercourse.

"Others, after a while, learn what works for them as a couple. I can only recommend that you take your time, get to know Gabriel again, and let nature take its course. Take it slow. When you're feeling up to it and are able to, go out on some dates. Spend time together doing what you both like. Don't put any pressure on your relationship because, unfortunately, your body has changed. Does that answer your questions and are there any others you want answers to?"

Fern tilts her head as if she is trying to go through the files in her head. Dr. Davids and I wait patiently, watching her closely but for different reasons. His reasoning is medical and mine is totally personal. I know Fern is feeling out of sorts with our *relationship*, or lack of it, but I haven't had time to even give it a thought. Never in all the time that she has been sick have I had the urge to go out and just fuck someone to fuck them. Look what happened when Katie tried to start something. Initially my body reacted, but my heart was never involved in whatever games Katie was playing. Fern is everything to me. Not saying my hand hasn't gotten a workout, because it has, but only with Fern in my thoughts.

"No questions. Lots of concerns. What happens if we can't get back what we had? Gabriel can only go so long without an intimate relationship." Fern's head goes down as she blushes. "He's a very physical man, Dr. Davids, if you know what I mean.

I lift her chin with my hand, gently caressing her cheek. "Sugar, I can go the rest of my life without sex as long as I have you. I know you're feeling out of sorts and being able to get out of here is putting all the doubts and questions forefront of your mind. Fern, think about it. How long has it been since we made love? It has been many months, honey, and I'm here every day with you, holding you, caressing you, and kissing you. Don't be upset, and pardon my language, but the fucking hall pass you spoke about to me before being admitted, to tell you the truth that was so hurtful, but I understood your intentions. Think you've been reading those books of yours too much. But to clear this up, no worries, and more importantly no expectations. If and when it does happen, I'm not on a schedule or anything."

Leaning into her whispering, I continue.

"Sugar, I've gotten good with my own hand. Don't you see the guns I am packin' due to all the extra workouts?"

Laughing, I give her a squeeze as she blushes even more, letting a small giggle out.

Dr. Davids sits patiently as we have our moment before he speaks up. "Okay, let's get back on track. Fern, you will go to the outpatient facility for approximately two to three weeks, and after that we'll reassess your progress. If all goes well within a month or so you can be back home."

Fern leans into me softly with wet eyes. Looking into those beautiful shining hazel eyes of hers, I fall more in love with her. She's the woman of my heart and dreams. I thank God every day that we have gotten this far. Pulling her close, with my arm around her shoulders, we sit on the couch listening to the next steps in getting Fern back at home and resuming our lives again.

(Fern)

Sitting in my small apartment in the outpatient facility, trying to concentrate on the book on my Kindle, my mind is caught between the past and present. Remembering all the things Gabriel and I did *back in the day* compared to what we are doing currently is so very different. My poor husband is in limbo with me. I'm not living, but not dead either. I know my depression is getting worse. That's why today Julie is coming over here so we can discuss what can be done. Crazy thoughts are in my mind as I try to figure out why Lydia died and I continue to live and breathe.

Getting back into my current read, when I get to the part where the girl gives in to the alpha male, I feel nothing. In the past I'd read these erotic stories and get hot and bothered. Now, nothing. It's like I am dead from the waist down. I try to recall how it felt to be with Gabriel. Putting my Kindle next to me, I let my mind drift and recall some of the times we were together, and even though it brings back beautiful memories, it does nothing to turn me on. Feeling the tears going down my face, I roll to my side, curling up into a fetal position, and start to rock back and forth as the realization that I may never get back to the way I was before because of all of these treatments and the transplant hits me. Having my own pity party, going deeper and deeper into myself, I don't hear the doorbell or the door opening until Julie's voice echoes into my subconscious.

"Fern, my God, what's the matter? Come on, honey, let me help you. Let's get you cleaned up."

Not comprehending at first as she moves me, I feel the warmth under me and the wetness in my pants. I can't believe I peed myself. As I try to clear the fogginess out of my head, the embarrassment takes over as I try to pull away from her.

"Fern, stop. There's nothing to be upset about. First, we get you washed up, then we talk."

As she gets me up, I instantly feel dizzy, grasping on to her to keep from falling down. She grabs the waistband of my pants to balance us both. Taking a deep breath, I try to relax until my body is under control.

After Julie gets me back to normal, we sit down at the table with cups of hot tea. She waits patiently for me to start, but I just don't know where to. Reaching across the table, she grabs my hands, squeezing them.

"There's nothing I haven't heard, Fern. You're driving yourself crazy for no reason. There is no right or wrong when trying to return back to your life. So much has changed for you and Gabriel, so don't think you're going to just walk back into your prior life. It doesn't work that way. We've talked about this. You're not out of the woods yet, so we want to try to stay away from stress. Yes, the stem cells took, and yes you are in remission, but your system is weak and anything especially upsetting can slow down the process and keep you from going home. You understand, don't you, honey?"

Nodding to Julie, her words penetrate deep inside of me. I should treasure this gift I have been given and not act like it's no big deal. I beat cancer and am one step closer to going home and having my happily ever after with Gabriel.

"Julie, I need help. Between the insecurities in my head and the depression, I feel so lost and alone. Please tell me how to fix this. I want my life back." Smiling, Julie claps her hands.

"Finally! Fern that is the best thing I've heard from you in a while. Now we are ready to bring it home. The insecurities are just you trying to catch up with real time. Depression is something that happens to the majority of people who have experienced such a traumatic event in their lives. You were fighting for your life. It takes your body and mind a while to realize and catch up that everything has worked out."

Taking a minute to gather my thoughts as Julie refills our tea, a calming feeling comes over me.

"Julie, I really want to fight for my recovery. So

whatever we need to do to stay on that path, please let me know. I've been pushing away the anti-depressive drugs because they scare me, but maybe I need something to keep from going to that dark place in my head. It drags me down and it gets harder each time to come back up. I'm ready to try and see if they will work for me. Like I told you before, I don't want to be on them forever, if it can be helped, but know I need help. Also maybe I can start moving around more, doing a bit of exercise or yoga. Something that will bring my body back to me. Right now it feels as if I am using someone else's body, as it doesn't feel like mine. I mean, I was never an exercise nut but tried to stay in shape as I started to age. Right now, not only am I a bag of bones, but have no muscle tone. Is this even possible?"

"Fern, definitely we will start with maybe some yoga as not only will that help with flexibility but also with your moods. Maybe we can get you a treadmill so you can start a walking program inside until you are able to walk outside. Right now it's too cold, but maybe by the time spring gets here you'll be ready to venture outdoors. Sound good?"

As we continue to plan my recovery, for the first time since I left the hospital, I feel good about my progress and more importantly, hopeful.

CHAPTER TWENTY-FOUR

PRESENT ~ WHAT ARE FRIENDS FOR? ~

(Gabriel)

Sitting in the lawyer's office waiting for them to enter, I look at Ann. These last weeks have really been hard on her. The loss of Lydia and the care of Charlie and Emma have worn her down. Actually, Trinity once again stepped up and has the kids currently staying with them to give Ann a break.

"You doing okay, Ann? Is there anything I can do for you?"

"No, Gabriel. You and your friends have been lifesavers for us. I don't even want to think where we would be if we had not met you. I'm just so tired all the time and worry so much about the babies, because let's face it, I'm just an old lady and can't keep up with them. I continue to wonder why God took Lydia and left me here with her children. They deserve so much more than me, Gabriel."

"I don't want to hear that negative shit, Ann. Those babies couldn't have a better person there for them. As we told you before, and we all mean it, family helps family and that's what all of you are to us. Have you gotten settled into the cabin? Do you like it? Let me know if you need anything or we need to change something."

"Oh my gosh, Gabriel, it is a slice of heaven. I can't believe that the beautiful little cabin is what I'm calling my home. My bedroom on the first floor makes it so much easier to function. Love everything about the kitchen. Can't wait to cook for Charlie and Emma when I'm feeling better. I wanted to make sure that it's okay we continue to stay there without Lydia? I would understand if plans changed because everyone worked so hard to give my daughter a place to raise her children and she's now gone."

Before she could continue, I butt in, "Damn it, Ann, knock it off. Sorry for my cussing, but you're family too, as are the kids. So knock it off, get yourself healthy, and enjoy your new home."

Just then the lawyer and two other people enter the room. He looks at both of us, extending his hand.

"Hi, John Bussels. You must be Ann and Gabriel. Please take a seat and we can get started. This is Tasha, my assistant, and Georgia is my paralegal."

After we all shake hands and take our seats, John continues, "Lydia contacted me right after she met you and Fern, Gabriel. She wanted to have a will drawn up.

Wait, didn't you want to Skype or FaceTime your wife for this?"

Grabbing the iPad from its carrying case. I nod.

"Sorry, John, actually forgot for a second. Give me a minute." I try to get the contraption working, but have no idea what I'm doing, even though Fern showed me numerous times.

As I start to get frustrated, Tasha reaches over, grabbing it from me, smiling. "Let me get to the program. What's your wife's name, Gabriel? Oh that's right, John said it was Fern, right? Let me connect us."

She starts pushing on the screen and then we hear a ringing. Finally I hear the connection.

"Hello, this is Fern. Gabriel, is that you? Thought you forgot about me."

Ann gives a soft laugh as I give her a look.

"Sugar, it's me. Hang on. Tasha, can I get that back, please?" Grabbing the iPad, I turn and look into my wife's eyes.

"Okay, sugar, let me introduce you. John is the attorney; Tasha is his assistant and Georgia is a paralegal. And Ann is right next to me."

"Hi. Nice to meet all of you. Ann, how you holding up, honey?"

I turn the iPad to Ann to answer Fern. "Doing okay, Fern. How about you?"

After they spend a minute or two catching up, I look to John. "Ready."

"Okay, let's get started. Fern, before you came on, I

had started to explain that Lydia contacted my office after she first met you before the transplant. She had many concerns about what would happen if something happened to her. Ann, your daughter spoke highly of you and never doubted you would do your best for them. But she understood your limitations and didn't want to burden you anymore than she already has. She told me that when she met you again, Fern, and really got to know you, she knew what she had to do. So I have a couple of letters here for all of you. I will give those to you to read privately. Now, I would like to read Lydia's final wishes."

Reaching for a stack of papers, he goes through them until he comes to single page.

"All right, I'm going to skip to the main part, if everyone is good with that. I have copies for everyone. This's Lydia's last will and testament and she was of sound mind and body. She leaves all of her personal possessions to her mom, Ann, with the understanding that anything sentimental will be put aside for her children when they are older. Also she has a small savings account and a money market which she couldn't remember the total amount but thought it had approximately $8,900.00 that she has not touched since before Charlie was born. It's the settlement from the lawsuit from her car accident. That said, the only item left is the custody of Charlie and Emma."

I start to feel something deep in my chest as I watch Ann squirm in her chair. Glancing my way, she shrugs her shoulders at me.

"Ann, your daughter loved you so much she

couldn't say enough about you and how your grandchildren adore you. She really struggled with this decision, but told me she needed to take care of her children first and foremost. That was her only thought. So her final request was that you, Ann, share joint custody with Fern and Gabriel of her two children, Charlie and Emma. That is if the Murphy's have no objections."

At first, I don't hear anything, then a small sniffle, then another until I know deep in my heart that my wife is crying. Turning the tablet around, I look at her trying to wipe the tears as quickly as they fall.

"Sugar, take it easy. Deep breath in and out. Come on, honey, no need to get upset."

I feel so lost because she is alone. She raises her head, eyes full, lips trembling, struggling to maintain eye contact.

I give her a moment, then speak to her, "Fern, what has you so upset? Lydia loved you in such a short time that she trusts her children in your care, or I should say, in Ann and your care. That's such an honor, sugar. You of all people understand how much Lydia loved her kids."

"Gabriel, she should be raising her children. I'm heartbroken that she's gone, but if this is her final wish, so be it. Ann, we'll never step on your toes and will only be there to back you up. I haven't gotten to know Charlie and Emma as much as Gabriel, but will treat them like they are our own."

"Fern, I have no worries or doubts. We will work

out the details when you're back home. The most important thing right now is that you continue getting better. Do it please, Fern, because I couldn't handle losing Lydia and you. Family is all Lydia cared about. Fern, you and Gabriel became part of her circle as you are in mine now too."

John finishes up with the particulars, asking Ann and I to sign a legal document stating we were present at the reading of the will, and I take a copy for Fern to sign. Ann also gets a list of all the items Lydia left which are meant for her children. Finally, the last sheet is a detailed list of the money Lydia had and that all goes to Ann. Shaking hands with John and the girls, I'm in shock. We now have two children we are sharing custody of. Not to mention the responsibility, which neither Fern nor I have any long-term experience with.

Walking outside behind Ann, she comes to a sudden stop.

"Gabriel, I will cash out the money Lydia left to me. Would you like me to give it to you or Des? You know, for the cabin. I know it isn't even close to what was spent, but I want to pay my share."

Shaking my head at her, I scowl in her direction. "Not happening, Ann. Keep the money either for you or for the kids. Everything has been taken care of, so no worries. Don't get all nuts on me either because eventually you'll need that money, so keep it safe. We're square."

Grabbing her close, giving her a hug, I feel her hanging on tight to me, not letting go. Giving her what she needs, I hold her, thinking how much this poor woman has gone through.

Finally, we part and after a brief conversation we each head to our cars. With everything in my head, the only place I can point my car to is Fern.

CHAPTER TWENTY-FIVE

PRESENT ~ TIME DOESN'T FLY BY ~

(Fern)

I have been in the outpatient facility now for twenty-two days and from what Dr. Davids is saying, I'm not going home anytime soon. My recent blood work showed some of my numbers were on the low side. I feel so let down because all I really want is to go home and try to get my life back with Gabriel.

"Fern, now don't get all melancholy. This is just a bump in the road to your recovery. So tell me, anything we need to talk about? How are you really feeling? Is that anti-anxiety drug helping you at all?"

"Sometimes it's helping and then other times I don't think so. My head seems to be clearer and the depression isn't so bad. I talked to the counselor and she recommended writing my thoughts down, so Gabriel brought a really pretty book for me to use. I guess this feeling of being in limbo is getting to me. I'm caught between not dying from the cancer and not being healthy enough to get back to my life. So I've just been taking it one day at a time. That's all I can do, right?"

"Let's increase the Xanax to a higher dose and see if that helps you. Also, I'm going to have you take an over-the-counter sleep aid, which will give your brain some time to relax. Continue with the counselor as long as you feel it is helping. I will check back with you in a couple of days after your next blood draw. And, Fern, you are doing a terrific job. Keep up the good work."

After he leaves, I look around my prison, as I refer to it when alone. It isn't a bad room/studio, but it isn't home. Gabriel and the guys have been killing themselves to get our house remodeled and I can't wait to see all that was done. Every time I ask my husband to take some pictures or even a small video, he makes an excuse and changes the subject, so I am getting suspicious of exactly what is going on in my house.

Going into the kitchenette, I put together a small lunch. I have no appetite but have to put something in my stomach so I can take my afternoon medication. Sitting at the small table, thinking about nothing in particular, I realize how truly alone I feel. This is worse than when I was in the isolation room.

I had Lydia there and now she's gone. I try to control my emotions, even though my heart is broken, I miss my friend. I am both scared and feel guilty. I'm scared that even though I have come this far, something is going to happen and I'll be joining her. What is worse is the guilt eating at me for surviving while she didn't. Lydia had so much more than me to live for. Those children, and she was a couple of months younger than me. Lost in my own head, I don't hear the door open or someone walking to me, so when Gabriel places his hand on my shoulder, I actually jump, screaming bloody murder.

"Holy crap, Gabriel, can you not be frigging sneak up on me like that? I almost crapped my pants."

"Sugar, what's got you all up in your head? I told you on that tablet thing that I was heading this way straight from the lawyer's office. Fern, look at me. What's the matter? Have you been crying?"

"Dr. Davids was here and I'm still on lockdown. Some of my numbers are low. He wants to change some of my crazy meds and add some sleep aid because he thinks that I'm not getting enough rest. I don't know why he thinks that because I do nothing but rest."

Looking at Fern, I hear her frustration and have just the job for her.

"Well, as you know we have been given the greatest gift from Lydia. Charlie and Emma are going to be spending time with us so," I drop the iPad on the table in front of her, "you need to start picking out the furniture and stuff that we'll be putting in their rooms at our house. Here's a list of what Ann shared that the kids like and here is our credit card. Go to town, sugar."

Raising her eyes to mine, Fern finally gives me that million-dollar smile of hers.

"Oh, Gabriel, you have no idea what you just did. Be prepared. I've been itching to do some shopping and this will definitely fill my day. Do you know which rooms you're going to put them in?"

As we discuss this new phase in our lives, I watch Gabriel, realizing how handsome he is. This is the first time since the transplant that I've actually looked at my gorgeous husband. He's bulked up even more, which seems impossible as Gabriel was a mammoth specimen of a man before. Wide shoulders, arms that are ripped, with a waist that is narrow, to nice, thick thighs. His wavy, auburn hair looks like it needs a trim, but I kind of like the look on him. It makes him appear softer compared to his shape. But his best features have always been those emerald-green eyes. They look into my soul and are always watching me. The look I give to Gabriel is in no way a sexual glance on my behalf. It's a woman recognizing her man. I've missed this feeling of just being with him.

"Sugar, what has you looking so serious? Come on, let's sit on the couch and watch something on TV. It has been a long day and all I want is you in my arms."

"That sounds fabulous, Gabriel. I love spending time with you like this. Just the two of us."

As we both stand to go to the small couch, he grabs my hand, squeezing while pulling me close. This right here is well worth everything I've gone through. To be able to enjoy this man in all his glory fills my heart and soul with hope for our future.

So we spend our evening cuddling on the couch, watching TV, just like a normal couple.

(Gabriel)

Looking at all the boxes and packages the UPS guy just dropped at the front door, I laughed out loud. Obviously, Fern didn't waste any time shopping for the kids. Opening the door, I greet the man.

"Morning. Is there more than that?"

"Half that truck is coming here, Mister. I have this here dolly to bring in the smaller boxes and packages, but might need a hand with the furniture boxes, if you don't mind. Partner called off sick today so I'm on my own. I can back the truck up on the grass to get it closer."

"Please don't drive on that grass. We just laid the sod a week ago and it was a pain in the ass. I'll help. Let me get some shoes on. Be right out."

As he drops the packages in the front room area then turns and walks out, I go to grab my shoes. Walking back out I'm shocked to see Cadence and Jagger carrying in a huge box.

"Where's this shit going, Doc?" Cadence yells.

"No idea. Not sure what's even in that box or any of the others. Let's stack them just to get them unloaded and then we can go through them. What are you both doing here?"

"Thought we would stop by to see if you want some

breakfast before we get started on painting the kids' rooms," Jagger explains.

As we make our way out the front door, carrying another huge box up the walkway is the UPS guy and Wolf, they walk past us to bring the box into the house. Damn, I'm getting a little anxious now thinking about the credit card I left with Fern. It has only been a little over a week and I know for a fact Trinity and Ann were over there helping her pick stuff out. Maybe I should have given this more thought. Oh well, as long as she had fun, the rest we can handle somehow.

"Morning, Doc. What, did you get a bug up your ass on the home shopping station?" Wolf asks with a grin.

"No, smart-ass, this shit, I mean stuff, is for Charlie's and Emma's rooms. I handed over the shopping to Fern and she took right to it, apparently. Let's get this all off the truck so this guy," I point to the guy struggling to hold his side of the box, "can go about his day." It takes them about forty-five minutes to unload all of the packages and boxes. I reach in my pocket, pull out a twenty, and hand it to the UPS driver.

"Thanks for putting up with us and getting this here in one piece. Have some lunch on me."

"Wow, thanks, sir. I truly appreciate it."

Shaking hands we part, him heading to his truck as I enter my house. Looking around, the guys have already started opening the big boxes. I look at a couple of different dressers, nightstands, what looks like a bed shaped like a car, and a princess bed. And these are just a small section of the mound of boxes in the room.

"So you guys busy this morning? Feel like helping me with all of this? Then we can work on getting this shit put together and finally set up the rooms. You in?"

Looking around they are all nodding their heads.

"Doc, you know we're always ready to give ya a hand. And it gets me out of my chores, so it's a win-win for me," Jagger finishes, giving me a huge smile.

"Okay, who needs some coffee? From what you said earlier no one has eaten, so let me throw some stuff together and then we can get started on the painting."

God, my shoulders are burning like a mother from the busy day of painting and all the unpacking, putting together, and moving of furniture. As we're finishing painting, the doorbell rang and when I opened it, another delivery guy informed me that he had a delivery for me. Not knowing what it was I asked.

"It's the jungle gym, tree house, and princess house you ordered."

Dumbfounded, I just point to the backyard as his partner starts unloading the truck. Cadence comes out, slapping my shoulder.

"Damn, Doc, she really went to town. Is this more shit we need to put together? Let them dump it in the backyard and let's finish up in the house first."

Going back in, we finish getting everything sorted

and put into either Charlie's or Emma's room. The bags and bags of clothes I left, hoping some of the girls would come by and help put them away. Looking at first Charlie's and then Emma's, I realize that Fern thought of everything. Each room is perfect and matches what Ann had told me the kids liked. At that moment I don't care how much this cost because looking at the rooms, I know Fern put her heart into this and that it brought her joy.

After another three hours in the backyard, putting everything together, we all were exhausted. I sent Jagger out in my vehicle to grab some pizzas. Picking up my phone I dial Fern.

"Hello?"

"Hey, sugar. How are you feeling?"

"Doing a bit better, Gabriel. I think the extra medicine is helping and I slept like a baby. I didn't wake up once. What are you doing? I haven't heard from you all day. You didn't have to work on a Saturday, did you?"

Hearing all the questions I know she is lonely. I feel horrible and know I should have gone to the outpatient facility to see her, but Dr. Davids told me to give her some alone time to start to manage on her own. This is another step to her moving on with her life. When she comes home, we have to act as normal as possible.

"Sorry, sugar, all of your orders came in today.

Thank God the guys were here as it took most of the day to get the walls painted, stuff put together, and everything where it needs to be. Also, the backyard looks like a kid's dream. Ann stopped by and loved everything. She said to tell you that you hit it right out of the park and the kids are gonna love everything. Once we eat, I'll come by for a bit. We can either play some cards or a board game, if you want."

"Hey, we'll come too. Actually, why don't we bring the pizza to Mom?" Cadence throws out from behind me.

"No, I don't want to be a pain. You guys are probably all exhausted. I'll just make something simple and will see you tomorrow, Gabriel." Then she hangs up.

I'm at a loss for words looking at the phone. Is this one of her "roid" moments?

"Did she hang up on you, Doc?" Wolf asks.

"Yeah, she did, and I don't understand why. I don't get it. She seemed fine, even sounded more like herself. Then all of a sudden abruptly she seemed panicked and hung up."

"Doc, are you the only one seeing her there?" Wolf inquires.

"Nope. Some of the girls have been by. Trinity, Ann, and Willow & Dee Dee I think."

"Maybe she's feeling lonely being that she is out of the hospital and no one is visiting like we did while she was in. Remember Dee Dee had the schedule so Fern was never really alone? Now she has all the time in the world and nothing to do. Maybe she needs the Horde to pick up her spirits. Just saying."

Thinking Wolf is on to something and knowing that Fern is fighting some really dark depression with her illness, Lydia's death, and just being alone, I agree with him.

"Got an idea, but need your help. I want to get everyone if they can to meet at Fern's in about forty-five minutes."

As I am speaking, Jagger walks in with the pizzas.

"Change of plans, Jag. We are going to Fern's place and have dinner. I'm going to pick up some chicken because she can't eat the pizza. If you'll explain to everyone what's going on, I'll meet you all there." Stopping at the door, I turn. "And thanks for all you guys did today and what you've been doing for Fern and me. Means the world."

Turning, I open the door and head over to surprise my wife.

CHAPTER TWENTY-SIX

PRESENT ~ SURPRISE ~

(Fern)

Hanging up on Gabriel was so uncalled for and rude, but crap, I'm stuck in this small little studio apartment while they are getting to have fun setting up everything for the children. Yeah, I picked it out and bought it, but still, it's not the same. Feeling bad about how I treated Gabriel, I pick up my phone and call our house. It rings and rings until the recorder picks up. I hang up wondering where he is.

I settle on the couch and pick up my tablet, opening my Kindle, looking to start a new book. There were quite a few that I haven't read yet, so I try to decide what I'm in the mood for.

Settling on Kristen Ashley, I'm torn between *Knight* and *Sweet Dreams*. Finally, I click on *Sweet Dreams* and start to read about Lauren and Jackson again. I instantly become so enthralled with their lives that I don't hear the knocking at my door at first. Then, as it gets louder, I figure Gabriel made the trip over here.

Getting up off the couch, I make the short walk to the door, opening it, and to my utter surprise see everyone standing there with big smiles on their faces. As they start to come in, I'm in shock and feel suddenly out of sorts. It's been ages since I was able to be in the same room with all of them without masks, gloves, and gowns. Since I have gotten here only Gabriel, Trinity, Ann, Dee Dee and Willow have visited.

As the rooms start to fill up, I finally see Gabriel in the very back, his arms filled with food bags. Reaching to help him, I am grabbed from behind and actually lifted off my feet. Letting out a yelp, I am moved to a chair and gently placed down into it. Looking up, I gaze into Cadence's twinkling black eyes.

"Take a load off, Mom. We got this. Relax and enjoy the company."

"Step away from her, Cadence. I'm in desperate need of a Fern hug," Wolf bellows from directly behind him.

"Hey, now, save some for me. It's been forever and I've a lot to catch Fern up on," Archie adds.

Being pulled this way and that way, a good half an hour goes by as I am hugged, kissed on, and coddled. At first, I feel a bit put out, but as I am desperate for human contact, each hug pulls me farther from that dark depression that I have been fighting.

Looking around the room I finally connect gazes with Gabriel, who is watching me intently. As we watch each other, everything else fades away and I feel something very foreign and strange happening. I'm getting that special feeling in my belly I used to get when he looked at me like that. Not nearly as intense, but I definitely am feeling some warmth in my belly and even have to catch my breath as I watch his eyes narrow as he realizes what's going on with me.

Then, he makes my heart beat a bit faster as he winks at me and gives me his sexy grin, which lights up his face. Dang, he's hot. Tatum Jackson in my book has nothing on Gabriel.

We're finally alone, and man, I am so frigging tired. "Gabriel, thank you, this has to have been one of the best nights I have had since this all started. Never laughed so much and now my belly hurts. You are one extraordinary man and I don't say that enough."

"Sugar, there isn't much I wouldn't do for you. I know this has been really hard on you and we've had some disconnect, so I'll say this, although you should already know it. I will always be here for you, support you, and love you. Always and forever, Fern. No matter what."

"I know that and have since before we got married, Gabriel. It just feels deep down like I'm alone. Truly alone, even in a room of people. I feel like no one sees the real me. That is, until you find me and complete me. Gosh, I am so tired. You must be exhausted."

Rubbing my eyes, I look around and notice that everything has been cleaned already. Thank God for the girls because I don't have the energy. Feeling Gabriel pull me close, my back to his front, I let out a sigh. I have missed this. This is my safe zone, where nothing or no one can hurt me. Lost in my thoughts, I don't notice anything until Gabriel clears his throat and moves slightly away from me.

"Ummm, sugar, let's get ready for bed. If you don't mind, I'll be spending the night. I'm too tired to drive back to our house."

"Sure, Gabriel. Why would I mind?"

Then, I realize why he pulled away as I push back and feel his erection against my back. *Well, hello there,* I think to myself. Then, I feel a rush of panic in my chest. What if he wants to have sex?

"Gabriel, you're always welcome here. I just thought you liked sleeping at home."

My voice betrays my nervous state and he gently turns me to face him. Looking in those emerald-green eyes of his instantly calms me and brings serenity over my body.

"Sugar, we knew this was going to come up, no pun intended." My gaze flies to his and I catch the twinkle in them. "Fern, let's sit and talk about this. I know this has been on your mind for some time now, and we need to address it. So come on, sugar."

We sit on the small couch next to each other, holding hands. He pulls me close and I smell his unique scent. It reminds me of vanilla, the great outdoors, and his musky scent all mixed up in one.

"Sugar, you know you can tell me anything. What's going on in that head of yours? Be honest."

Not knowing where to start, I hem and haw until it is too apparent that my nerves have gotten the best of me. Feeling Gabriel reach for me, I let out a grunt, yeah a grunt, as he pulls me into his lap. Wrapping me up in those massive arms of his, feeling the goose bumps from his breath on my neck, he leans in, his mouth touching my ear.

"Let it out, Fern, 'cause I ain't going anywhere. We can't move forward until we leave our fears behind."

"Gabriel, you know I love you with my entire heart. Always have. Since all of this started, I don't have the feelings I used to." Hearing him gasp I realized what I just said. "No, Gabriel, not about you..." I whisper awkwardly, "about sex."

I feel the relief in his body as he sighs. "That's it, baby? I'm not worried about that at all."

"Well, darn it, I am. How can you act like it isn't a big deal? We haven't made love, in what, almost ten or eleven months. Jesus, let's just call it almost a year. I know you, and sooner or later you'll get sick of this and move on to someone who wants to touch you, be touched, and have huge amounts of sex."

After my outburst I can feel the almost scary vibe coming off my husband, but I say nothing, just let it sit and wait for it to happen.

"Fern," he starts as he moves me to sit on the couch away from him. "If that's what you think of me, then there is no us. Sex has never been the 'all' of us. It was phenomenal and awe-inspiring, but I've told you time and time again, especially since your cancer, that if we don't ever have sex again it wouldn't matter to me. Shit, I mean it would bother me because of the closeness and intimacy, but I love you, Fern. All of you—the good, bad, healthy, and sick. I know this is heavy on your mind but try to let it go. We need to rediscover each other. That's what I'm going to do and not compare to what was but what can be. Okay, sugar? Can you do that? For me?"

Nodding my head, I hear the voice that has been missing since I got sick. The voice that makes me weak in the knees.

"Fern, I need to hear your answers."

His deep baritone gives me shivers. I'm shocked because I haven't felt anything remotely like this it seems like forever. And holy moly did I miss it.

"I can do that for you, Gabriel. Yes, I can." Clearing my throat of the lump there, I shake my hair out of my face.

"It feels like something died in me. There has never been a time in the past when I looked at you and my belly didn't feel like butterflies were there, or the shiver that goes up my back at your voice. Now nothing happens. It's like we lost our connection. I mean, we have lost that special thing we had and it's my fault. I don't have any sexual feelings or desires and am literally tearing myself apart knowing eventually that you'll need more than it seems than I can offer.

"I don't want you to stay with me because you pity me but because you want to." Lowering my eyes, as I don't want to see his, I wait. And wait. And wait.

Finally, he cups my chin, raising my head, making me look at him. What I see there... Oh my God. The look in his eyes is pure and unadulterated desire. His eyes glow from within and that dominant male is awakening to a challenge. I see it all with one glance.

"Sugar, what did we decide many years ago? Our intimate relationship was ours and ours alone. We don't name it or try to be like others. We are unique. We only worry about each other. No, we don't claim to be into BDSM and all that goes with that title, but I have a very dominate personality, especially in our bedroom, and you're such a sweet submissive personality as you want to please me at all times.

"Even now, all you are worried about is pleasing me. Not how it works, Fern. We have been down this road too many times over the years. I'm going to go take a quick shower and I want you to really think about the years we've been together. We have definitely had our ups and downs, but one thing holds firm. Our ability to keep our lines of communication open. I'll be back, sugar."

After Gabriel leaves the room, I sit back and do what he asked. Trying to remember how we managed over all these years to have such an intense relationship, even with all the disappointing moments we have shared. One memory stands out above all others. It was just after we were married, both young, and I was naïve in many ways. Gabriel wanted to surprise me, so we were on our way to a friends of his. As we approached the large home, surrounded by a security fence, my breath caught in my throat.

"Gabriel, where are we going?"

"Sugar, do you trust me?"

"Always, Gabriel, but may I ask a question?" He nodded. "Does this have something to do with what we spoke about last week? About what I found on the computer?"

His whisper of a laugh sent chills down my spine. Dang, what has he gone and done? The week before, while playing on the computer, I came across an article about BDSM. My interest was piqued as I read about something I thought was made up. The article gave links to informational sites, which I read through like a hungry wolf. Finally when Gabriel came home that night, I'd brought up the subject and he'd just sat there, those penetrating emerald-green eyes watching. When I'd finished, we'd just sat looking at each other.

"Fern, are you happy with our lives? What I mean is, are you satisfied with our sex life?

Embarrassed but knowing he wanted an answer, I'd nodded in agreement.

"No, Fern. I need to hear you."

"Yes, Gabriel. I am happy. You're the only man I have ever wanted or needed and have been with, as you know."

"So what's the fascination with BDSM, then?"

"When I was reading the article and they described the dominant alpha male, I felt like they were describing you. Not in a bad way, but the way you always take care of me and not just sexually. I feel safe with you and that was brought up in the article too. They talked about how the relationship in BDSM is so much more defined due to the communication and total honesty aspect."

His eyes had seemed more intense to me and his body even bigger, like he'd taken a breath and it expanded in his muscles.

"Fern, sugar, I think it's time we have a discussion if you're up to it."

That is when my husband, and the only man I have ever been intimate with, explained to me that he had dominant traits and liked to be in control. Gabriel went through a long explanation and after we even tried some things, he told me that he had wanted to do some of them for a long time. Some I liked, others not so much. The most enjoyable one was when he held me down or tied me up. I liked him having all the control. It made me feel safe. Little did I know where this would have us going on a Friday night.

That night forever changed our relationship for the better. If I hadn't trusted Gabriel to the utmost, who knows where we would be today. He was right, again. We have been through so much over the years and the one thing that kept us strong was our communication. We didn't keep secrets from each other, ever. Remembering how honest my Gabriel was about the problem with the energy drinks and over-the-counter pills. He just told me the other day he is finally feeling like all of the side effects were gone. Then not wanting to think about it but his honesty about Katie and the episode in our own home. He could have hidden it but he didn't. He was honest and told me what happened, and more specifically, how he reacted at first. That made me feel so bad because he had a sexual reaction to another woman. But after thinking on it, I realized any man would.

Their bodies are so different than ours. They are visual beings and that is all it takes to get a 'rise' out of them. That thought has a giggle escaping my lips. Where for women we need some form of emotional connection to a man. Rubbing up to me does nothing but that same man helps me in some way, treats me nicely, then brushes up to me, things are different. Dang, I am such a fool.

Finally realizing what Gabriel is trying to do here my heart beats a bit faster and I feel something that has been missing forever. Hope. Hope for a closer relationship with Gabriel, whatever that turns out to be.

As if on cue, he walks back into the room in only a towel wrapped around his slim waist. His hair is a tousled mess, as his eyes never leave mine. Gosh, the self-confidence radiates off of him. He sits so close to me; our hips and thighs are plastered together. He doesn't say anything, just sits there with me, only our thighs touching.

"Gabriel, what are we doing? I'm not ready for sex, not even with you. I don't want you to see what my body has become. It isn't attractive. I'm a bag of bones and have scars everywhere, not to mention the scars from the sores."

Grabbing my hand, he pulls me closer. "Sugar, I'm not asking for anything from you, but you're wrong. You are attractive to me. Always will be."

He moves my hand to between his legs and I feel his hard cock under the towel. "Does this feel like I'm not attracted to you? Honey, anytime we're in the same room this happens. But I also know you aren't there yet and I'm good with that. As I said before, my hand has been getting a workout and it only works because I have a mental image of you that I bring up every time I take care of myself."

My hand seems to have a mind of its own as it tightens on his cock with the thought of him pleasuring himself. He takes in a deep breath. "Fern, baby."

Something inside me likes the feeling of power as I hold his steel hard cock in my hand. I squeeze it at first, then start to slowly move up and down the length of him and he lies back, never making any attempt to touch me, which I appreciate.

The towel shows a wet spot were Gabriel must be

leaking precum, so I remove my hand and the noise he makes tells me he's disappointed until I pull the towel apart, allowing his cock to spring up at full mast. I take in a deep breath. This is the first time I have seen *him* since before my transplant. God, I did miss this closeness. Running my fingers around the large vein under the rim, he jerks his hips up. I close my hand around his girth and start a steady rhythm with a twist around the bulbous, purple head. He pumps his hips with every pull and yank of my hand as his breathing becomes shallow.

"Fern, I'm not going to last, sugar. It feels so fucking good. Your small hand around me. It's so damn soft and cool on my goddamn hot cock. Go faster and harder, baby. Please, don't stop. I need this so bad. I've missed you, Fern. God, how I've missed you."

As I watch my husband unravel, I continue giving him a hand job, feeling his cock grow even harder in my hand moments before he lets loose and streams of white cum propel out of his cock, onto his six-pack stomach. For the first time in a long time, I feel like a desirable woman.

CHAPTER TWENTY-SEVEN

PRESENT ~GETTING BACK TO LIFE~

(Fern)

It has been almost week since Gabriel and I had our *'special'* time together. He didn't try to push himself on me in any way, but something changed in me. No, I didn't mysteriously have my sex button turned on, but I feel more comfortable in my body. I've even spoke to my counselor about it and she told me that everyone is different, but time changes everything. She explained that I need to trust not only in Gabriel, but also myself.

So, with the help of Dee Dee and Trinity, I'm nervously sitting in the chair at a hair salon as the stylist looks at my hair that has grown out over the last couple of months. It is a mess of all different lengths and colors, but from my scalp to about three inches down it has grown out and is showing my natural color. Getting the go ahead from Dr. Davids, I am giving the stylist free rein to cut and color my hair. It has been such a long time since I've done anything like this and it feels strange.

Watching Trinity getting some temporary color (because of her pregnancy) put into her long blonde hair, I am so undecided on what to do.

Looking over to my left, Dee Dee is getting her nails done. This is their treat to me—a day of beauty. As I try to relax, my cell phone starts ringing. Reaching for my purse, pulling it out, I see Gabriel's number.

"Hey, Gabriel. What's up?"

"Sugar, just checking in. How is your day of beauty going? Not that you need it."

I laugh at his comment, which is so full of BS. "Yeah, right, husband. Remind me to make you an appointment to get your eyes checked. Going okay, not sure what to do, but will work it out. Will you be by later?"

"Planning on it, but the garage is busy and Des wants to have a staff meeting tonight. Been having some problems here and Des wants it straightened out."

As we finish our conversation, the stylist comes over and we try to decide what to do with my hair. I like Daniel, the stylist, and finally after about fifteen minutes of going back and forth, I put it in his capable hands.

"Daniel, as long as my hair is not a rainbow color and standing on end, please just do what you think is best. If Dee Dee trusts you, I know I'm in good hands."

After what seems like hours later, my hair is cut and colored and my fingers and toes are a pretty shade of pink. I even let Trinity and Dee Dee talk me into having my eyebrows shaped and some makeup put on my pale face. Then, they turned me to look in the mirror. When I see what was done, I break out instantly into tears. Both girls run to my side, hugging me, telling me it's all right, it can be changed if I don't like it. Trying to catch my breath, it takes me a moment or two.

"No, it isn't that I don't like it, I love it. It just shocked me. I haven't looked human in a long while and when Daniel turned me around, I realized that I'm not a bad looking woman."

Both Dee Dee and Trinity bust out laughing, as do Daniel and his assistant. Finally realizing what I just said out loud, I too join in the laughter. That is until a throat clears in the background, and we all come to a complete stop. Standing in the doorway of the salon are Gabriel and Des. But all I see is him. His emerald-green eyes are on fire and his body seems tense and ready to pounce.

I watch as he looks me up, then down, then up again. As our eyes meet, he mouths, "Wow," and then winks. Everyone laughs, but to me it's only Gabriel and me in the room. I slowly approach him, watching his reaction. Something deep down in my tummy feels warmed by his admiring sexy look.

"What are you doing here, Gabriel?"

"Des wanted to check on the girls and I came along

for the ride, hoping to catch a glimpse of you. And what a glimpse I got. Damn, Fern, you look hot. I mean... you're so beautiful.

I giggle at his discomfort as he pulls me closer, giving me a very tight hug. He pulls me in so close I can feel his cock hardening right against my stomach.

"Gabriel, really? Here and now?" I ask, as I can imagine the blush covering my face.

"Sugar, when you look like you do right now, be thankful that's all that is happening."

Watching him watch me, I smile suddenly. Somehow, I know things are going to be just fine with us, no matter how much time I need. Gabriel will always be there for me.

"Babe, we got to get back, but I want to take you out tonight. Let's say a late dinner, if that's okay? I'll call when I leave the garage so you can be ready. That work?"

"Yeah, honey, it actually does work perfectly. And thank you."

At my endearment his head shoots up and momentarily he looks lost, almost, but immediately his eyes warm and he pulls me to him for a kiss that would have started some timbers on fire. Releasing me, he cups my cheek softly. "Love you, sugar."

"I love you too, Gabriel."

As I watch him follow Des out, I feel at peace for the first time in almost a year. Each day I feel stronger and more confident. I am finding things out about myself through the counseling sessions too. All in all, my life is good and I can't wait for the next phase to start. I have something to share with Gabriel tonight that Dr. Davids revealed to me today during his visit. Our lives are about to be back on track.

Turning to get my stuff together, I hear a strange laugh behind me. Looking back I see Katie staring at me with a strange glare.

"Wasn't that so sweet? You and Gabriel all snuggled together. Too bad it won't last, Fern."

Not in the mood for her mean ways, I look her up and then down. "Not sure why it is any of your business what my husband and I do, but this is your only warning, Katie. Stay away from Gabriel. I mean it."

"What are you going to do, Fern, if I don't? Or should I say, *sugar*?"

I feel anger in my body heating my face at her sarcasm on Gabriel's nickname for me. I move forward to get in her face, but to my utter surprise Trinity beats me to it.

"Bitch, step back now. Don't you ever talk to my mom like that again, you hear me? I'm done with your shit. I've always respected my elders, but you are testing my patience. Now move along."

Katie has a look on her face that scares me, but Trinity either doesn't see it, or it doesn't bother her. As the older woman approaches the younger one, all hell breaks loose as Dee Dee gets in the middle.

"As Trinity told you, Katie, get the hell out of here before you regret it. I'm not going to let you treat Fern the way you treated me. It isn't going to happen, so get out now."

Laughing, Katie throws her blonde hair back, hands on her hips. "Do you really think either of you intimidate or scare me? You're all bitches. And you," pointing at me she continues, "are a sick, dying hag who has that man tied in knots. I'm trying to do you a favor by taking care of him. And you, Dee Dee, I've been there with Des so we could share what really gets him off. You know he likes it rough and being in control, right? Trinity, sorry haven't been with Cadence, but shit so many others have I'm sure we can find you some help. That boy can go for hours and from what I hear, those piercings are fantastic. The three of you think you're better than me, but really you're not. I know how to take care of a man, unlike any of you."

Katie has drawn a crowd not only from the salon but in front of the building with people looking in. I'm so embarrassed but won't let her push me around anymore.

"Katie, you're just the town tramp and everyone knows it. You're like an airport runway with so much traffic in and out. You might think you can take care of a man, but I don't see any sticking around you and that in itself says something."

At my words both Dee Dee and Trinity start laughing, as do some of the people in the salon. Katie actually growls, then comes toward me, but before she reaches me, an arm wraps around her waist stopping her. Looking up I see a furious Des behind her, his arm pulling her back until he turns, swinging her aside like a doll. Katie stumbles, almost falling until Gabriel catches her hand, pulling her short. As soon as she seems to have her balance, he immediately lets her go, coming toward me to pull me close.

"Bitch, what the fuck did I tell you the last time you approached Dee Dee with your fuckin' lies? Do you not remember?"

Katie actually pales at the harshness in Des's tone.

"Des, I didn't do anything. We were just talking. No harm, I swear. Come on, let's go talk this out. I can explain, babe, just give me a minute or two."

Hearing a disgusted noise, I see Cadence coming toward Trinity. He looks her up then down and turns to Katie. "You have been a pain in our asses forever. Get it through your thick motherfuckin' head that you and Des had nothing. It wasn't a relationship. It was plain and simple fuckin'. He used you to relieve a need and from the way he tells it, wasn't that great. But when you can get it and don't need to work for it, you take what you can get. Don't ever speak to my wife, mother, or Dee Dee again, bitch. I'm not Gabriel or even Des, Katie. It won't matter to me that you're a bitch in heat 'cause next time I'll deal with you first, then talk after. Get me?"

"Did you just threaten me, Cadence Powers? Because if you did, I have witnesses and I will definitely press charges."

As she looks around, not one person meets her

glance and we hear some of them saying, "Didn't hear a thing" as they turn to leave.

Katie stomps her feet as she lets a loud scream out. "I don't get it. What is so special about these hags? They don't have anything I don't, so why?" She runs her hands through her hair.

"Class, self-respect, self-esteem, and inner beauty, brains besides being gorgeous. That's what they have, Katie." We all turn to see Wolf and Axe standing at the doorway and are amazed at Wolf's comments.

"You might be a good-looking woman, Katie, but you've a black heart and everyone sees it. Look at the mess you started here. Might want to move on as I called the sheriff and he's on his way. Abusing and physically threatening a woman who's been fighting cancer with witnesses around will get you arrested."

She hesitates for a moment, then moves toward the door just as Des does. Stopping short, she looks at him and I realize that Katie is actually in love with Des. Feeling a moment of pity for her, I remember what she has done to Des and Dee Dee and the moment passes quickly.

"Katie, this is it. No more. Cadence's words are true. I never felt anything for you. It was fuckin' and that's it. Think about it, I never took you out or went to the movies, dinner or nothing because you weren't worth my time. When I needed the release, I called, you answered, and we fucked. End of story. Get over it."

Katie seems to crumble from his words. Watching

his face as he speaks, her eyes actually fill with tears and when Des finishes, she immediately opens the door and leaves. I get the feeling we won't be seeing her any longer.

(Gabriel)

Finally this day is over. Hopefully we're done with the Katie bullshit drama after that confrontation at the salon. All I have to get through is this staff meeting and then I get to take my Fern out.

Damn, I almost swallowed my tongue when I got my first glimpse of her in that salon. Her hair was cut in short layers to frame her face and the colors were so soft and shiny. I loved the browns and golden blonde streaks, I guess you would call them. Then when she got closer, I noticed the pink fingers and toes, which made me harder the longer I looked. The light makeup complemented her features and all in all she was my Fern, but wasn't. This new Fern looked healthy and sexy.

All the procedures, chemotherapy, and radiation had taken its toll on her and today was the first time I have seen her look healthy in months. God, I wanted to push her up against the receptionist desk and have my way with her. But unfortunately, that isn't happening anytime soon. We're nowhere near that, or maybe I should clarify

Fern isn't ready for that. Personally, I could go at any time, seeing as I'm hard as steel whenever I am around my wife. But Fern needs time and I have held myself back so I don't scare her. Since the hand job she gave me last week, she has touched me more and she gave me another one later that week. She made sure I didn't touch her in an intimate way at all and as soon as I came, she moved quickly away. I get the feeling that even though she wants to do this for me, she also feels like it's an obligation. That's one thing I want to talk to her about tonight.

"Let's get this started so we can all go home," Des bellows out.

As we all take a seat, Des grabs some papers and leans against the counter. "All right, really quick... business has been picking up since that other garage in town closed down. With everything going on, we're shorthanded and I wanted your input. Got a couple of applications so let's get down to it. First up is Jagger, Dee Dee's son. He's still in school, obviously, but would like to work nights and weekends. His skill set is none but he's a quick learner. He would shadow Cadence and Archie in the shop. Any nays on him?" Looking around, Des nods his head.

"We'll let him know tonight he's gonna be so excited. Next, we have two applicants to work with Wolf and Gabriel on the bikes. We know both of these guys already; they're relocating to our area and need some work. They are Enforcer from the Intruders and Ugly from the Asphalt Riders." I can't believe the guys are leaving their MCs to move here. Wonder what's up. Des continues on.

"I know you're wondering why these guys are moving here and that isn't our business. I have been told both are going Nomad. Any issues with either of these guys?" Again no one says anything.

"Okay, last thing on my agenda. Registers have been coming up short here and there. I don't want to start making assumptions or accusing anyone, but it stops now. I'll overlook what has been taken already, but if it continues, be aware I will prosecute to the full extent of the law. There's no reason to steal as everyone in here would help anyone if they needed it. So get your shit together and knock it off. Got it?"

I look around the room, trying to figure out who it could be, and I stop on the newer guy, Tommy. His head is down while his cupped hands are shaking. Guilty as hell. Looking up at Cadencem he sees it too and nods to me.

"All right, let's get the hell out of here. Everyone have a good night, be safe if you are ridin'. See y'all in the a.m." Des goes to Dee Dee, grabbing her as they walk hand in hand out of the front waiting area to his office.

Glad this shit is over. I pull out my cell, scrolling to Fern's number. Ring one, ring two...

"Hello?"

"Hey, sugar, you feelin' good enough to grab a bite to eat?"

"Yes, Gabriel. I'm ready and waiting." Her voice seems full of excitement. Nice to hear.

"Okay, let me stop at home, wash up, change, and I'll be there, say thirty to forty-five minutes."

"Perfect. I'll be waiting and, husband, I have something to share with you. Can't wait."

After one of my quickest showers ever, I put on some clean jeans and a Henley. For April it's brisk tonight, so on the way out I grab a jacket. I need to spend some time on the house, clean it up a bit, and I still have some of the packing shit from when the guys were over helping with the kids' rooms. They haven't spent any overnights yet but have stopped by here and there to visit and check out their rooms. Which they loved, both of them.

Driving to the outpatient facility, traffic is heavy, so it takes the full forty-five minutes.

CHAPTER TWENTY-EIGHT

PRESENT ~ THE DAY HAS ARRIVED ~

(Gabriel)

My eyes keep going to Fern, looking her up and down. Damn, this woman—she takes my breath away. This is the first time since before the charity ride that she looks truly healthy. She has color in her cheeks and the cute dress with heels is making my dick hard, which isn't exactly a good thing for me. Got to get it under control. I don't want to freak out my wife while sitting at a restaurant.

"Sugar, is that dress new? I don't recall seeing you in it before?"

"Yes, Gabriel, it is. I went with Dee Dee before we went to the salon and found it. You like?" she asks in a flirty voice. My entire body reacts to that voice.

"Darlin', I wish I could show you just how much I enjoy that dress. Let's just say it's gettin' a rise out of me."

Giggling, Fern's cheeks turn a pretty pink as she

looks at the menu. I'm beyond thrilled that it appears that she is feeling better. I missed this side of her.

"Do you know what you are getting, husband?"

"Sugar, same as always. I'm in a chop house. I get steak. How about you?"

"I'm torn, Gabriel. I'd kill for a steak, but not sure my body can take it. Sick of chicken and not feeling fish. Doesn't leave a lot."

Watching her, my heart rate increases. God, she's my everything. As always, I have to fix everything in her life.

"Okay, sugar let's do this—I'll get the larger steak so you can have some of that and then get some chicken or maybe pasta, but do something different. Order an entree you are dying to try and haven't as of yet. If you don't like it, I'm a garbage disposal, so I'll just give you more steak and will eat your food. That work for you, sweetie?"

Nodding her head she giggles softly. "You're always my hero, Gabriel, fixing everything. Thank you."

"Never doubt it, Fern, as long as I have breath in me, I'll always have your back."

Just then the waitress returns, asking about drinks. I see Fern's face fill with alarm and dread.

"Do you have bottled water?" The waitress replies yes. "Great, give us to start two bottled waters over ice. Throw in lemon slices please. Bring the bottle here and open it here, if you don't mind? Then I'll have a draft beer and my wife will have a hot tea with honey. Right, Fern?"

Nodding her head, I look back at the waitress.

"We're ready to order, too." After placing our order, the waitress goes back to get our drinks as I pull Fern closer to me.

As we catch up on our day, I feel like this is going to be a perfect night, and without a doubt, Fern deserves many, not just one. Thinking about our earlier conversation when I checked in with her, I wait for the waitress to bring our drinks and then I look to my wife.

"All right, now that's out of the way, what's your good news, sugar? I sure can use some. Give it to me." Trembling with excitement and nerves, I try to control my breathing.

"Gabriel, today Dr. Davids came to see me again. After we spoke about some things that have been bothering me, he gave me the okay." She looks across the table, reaching for my hands before going on. "Husband, I'm finally coming home."

My head shoots up as I look at my loving wife, who has the most breathtaking smile on her face.

Feeling as if my lungs stopped working, I look at Fern—who is smiling huge—as I finally comprehend what she's telling me. Hearing the words I actually didn't know if I would ever hear, my body's in shock. It all comes barreling at me. We made it. No, Fern made it.

She beat the fucking cancer. We have our lives back. As she watches me, the smile starts to fade. I need to get my head out of my ass because this is fantastic news.

"Sugar, holy shit! Thank God. That is such phenomenal news. When can you come home? Did Dr. Davids give you any restrictions? Do we have any idea of what type of regimen he is going to put you on? Will there be a visiting nurse like you have right now?"

She raises her hand at me. "Gabriel, stop, I can't keep up with you. First calm down. You're as pale as a ghost. Take a couple of breaths. Drink some water, please. I don't need you passing out. Now to answer some of your questions, he said he wanted to meet with both of us at the hospital, day after tomorrow, to go over everything he thinks we will need to know.

"I know that nothing has changed so no fresh flowers, no fruit or vegetables unless cooked, no well water, and we still can't bring the cats home. Besides that, the rest he will go through with us."

As we discuss her homecoming, my mind is running in so many directions. I need to get a hold of the girls and get them to help me get the house cleaned up, fridge packed with food Fern can eat, and let everyone know the day has arrived. My Fern is coming home.

Off in my own head, I feel her hand squeeze mine as she clears her throat. "Where did you go, Gabriel? I know this has been rough on you, honey, but it's over now. We can go back to our lives. Are you happy?"

As I go to reply, here comes the waitress with our

food. Well, some food, not sure whose. As she brings salads to the table, I look at Fern who is frowning. Definitely not what we ordered. When she goes to put the plates on the table, I grab her attention. After clearing up that mess, knowing we didn't order salad as that is one of the items Fern is still unable to eat, I settle back in and glance at Fern, who's watching me closely.

"Sugar, what's going on in your mind? I can see the wheels moving. This is one of the happiest nights of my life, knowing you will be back home. We're truly blessed so there is nothing you can say that will change how I feel."

"Gabriel, I'm so happy to be coming home. But we still have some issues that need to be dealt with."

She looks around to make sure no one can hear her. "I am still so unsure of myself and we have been getting closer, a bit more intimate recently, but my body isn't what it was and a lot of the feelings haven't returned, so I just don't want to be a disappointment to you, Gabriel."

Knowing exactly where she is going with this, I try to find the right words to explain.

"Sugar, look at me. Come on, Fern, really look at me. We have been through so much over the years so you know that even though, like every other red-blooded male, I love sex, it's not something that is necessary for me to live.

"You have been really sick now—for what—three quarters of a year or maybe even closer to a year, and until you were in this outpatient facility there has been no sexual interaction. Have I treated you differently? No, because that is what love is, Fern. Love is not sex. I love you, however I get you. So yes, we have issues, but nothing spending time and getting to know each other again won't cure. I told you then we will work it out. Intimacy is not only intercourse it is whatever we want it to be. So get that shit out of your head, especially tonight because, sugar, I can't wait to get you back to your room so we can sit on the couch, cuddle, and make out like we did when we were teenagers. That, Fern, is all I want. No expectations. You good?"

Watching her watch me, I wait impatiently to see what she's going to do. I know this is hard on her and she is worried about the sex stuff, but truthfully, I just want her home to sleep next to and cuddle with in our bed. Whatever else happens is a bonus.

Finally, she smiles a brilliant smile directly at me. "Okay, Gabriel, we will do this your way. I just wanted to make sure you understood where I'm at with this. You know I'm seeing a counselor. Maybe you should come with me a time or two, so we can work on this together and set our expectations on what each of us wants or needs. But tonight I'm with you, honey, I want to feel your arms around me as we plan for this next journey in our lives. I love you, Gabriel Murphy."

"Back at you, Fern Murphy. Sugar, I'll always love you. Forever and a day."

CHAPTER TWENTY-NINE

PRESENT ~ GETTING BACK TO NORMAL ~

(Gabriel)

Damn, I didn't realize all the shit that was involved with Fern coming home. Dr. Davids and Julie both had page after page of instructions in a binder to go over with us. My wife was so exhausted after our meeting going over everything, she fell asleep halfway back to the facility. I now have my work cut out for me. We all decided that this weekend would be Fern's homecoming. So being Tuesday, I have four days to get everything ready.

After she told me last night, I made one call. I called Dee Dee to let her know the phenomenal news. She then passed the word around and this morning before I even left, the house was filled with people there to organize and clean the house. Daisy made sure all of the cleaning supplies were natural after reading up on the subject. Willow and Archie also showed up with Prudence, all having their jobs already from Dee Dee. I had nothing to worry about.

As I drove, my mind went back to what the doctor explained to us. Fern is doing very well but we need to be careful. No one who is sick is allowed over and any kids that are at the house can't even have the sniffles. Julie also explained that going home could actually depress Fern because of all the time she missed. Everyone is going to have to keep an eye on her. We went through the dos and don'ts with Julie. A visiting nurse would come over the first couple of days so Fern could settle. I checked with Des and took a couple of vacation days so we could do this together. I didn't want Fern by herself. She seems a bit unsure of herself today.

"Gabriel, what's on your mind? You look upset about something," Fern asks as she stretches in the passenger seat.

"Nothing's wrong, sugar, just running through everything that has be done for Saturday. Now that you're awake, do you want a quiet return home or a welcome party?

Looking her way, I see the fear in her face. Well, got my answer. "No worries, Fern, we will do quiet and maybe Sunday if you are feeling up to it, some of the Horde can stop by."

We talk about everything and nothing while I drive back to the outpatient facility. Just as I go to park the truck, my phone goes off.

"Hello?"

"Gabriel, is that you?"

"This is Gabriel. Who's this?"

"It's Ann and I have a huge problem. I have to go in overnight for a sleep test and Trinity isn't feeling well with the pregnancy. I didn't know who else to call but need someone to watch Charlie and Emma."

Damn. Can't bring the kids here by Fern, we're too close to her getting out.

"Ann, give me some time, I'll find a babysitter for them, if that is okay. I'm with Fern and, unfortunately, can't bring them near her yet."

We say our goodbyes and I look to see Fern already on her cell.

"Hey, Archie, it's Fern. Yes, doing well, thank you. I need a favor from Willow and you, if possible. Ann needs an overnight babysitter. Yeah, both Charlie and Emma. You don't mind? Great, can you girls go to the cabin, as it won't upset the kids because they're home? Okay, we will let Ann know and Archie...thanks, sweetie."

She looks my way with a huge smile on her face and I catch my breath. This is the Fern I remember, always taking care of everyone and everything. It seems like Momma Fern is back.

Later that evening, after leaving Fern, I arrive home to a dozen or so cars and trucks in the drive and parked on the street. Every light is on in our house and I can hear music and voices as I head up the walkway. As I swing the door open, my shock has to show on my face. The house looks frigging beautiful. Better than *Better Homes and Gardens*. The new hardwood floors are shining and all the furnishings are placed to best show off all the work we have done here. Looking around at everyone, who as of yet haven't seen me, I am momentarily stunned at how quickly my life is changing again. For a brief moment I crave an energy drink, but then push that thought out of my mind. I'm finally feeling normal again. I'm never, and I mean never, going down that road again.

As I watch the Horde work, something catches my eye to the corner. Daisy seems to have isolated herself from everyone and is working on a sign of some sort. Really looking at the young girl, I am shocked at how pale and drawn she looks. Her eyes find mine and I see the pain in them before she hides that look that makes me immediately worry. *What's going on with her?* I think to myself. I really need to speak to Dee Dee about that.

Finally, one by one, they notice me and we catch up on the day's events. I explain to them that Fern would rather come home on Saturday and just chill, not wanting anyone to make a big deal of it. After much back-and-forth, everyone agrees to do what is best for Fern. We discuss the options for Sunday and come to the conclusion that it would be very relaxed so everyone can drop by whenever they want and just say hi.

Closing the door after Jagger, the last to leave, I'm exhausted. Going to the fridge, I grab a beer and head out to the back patio, sitting on of the loungers. I take a long drag on my beer, taking a minute to just absorb the day. I know they worked their asses off here to finish up everything, get the furniture back in the house from the remodel, and just clean. Tomorrow Dee Dee and Trinity are going shopping with the list of food that Fern can eat and what can't be in the house.

Looking up at the dark sky covered in stars and a half crescent moon, I take in a deep breath. Closing my eyes briefly, trying to calm myself, I take a couple of breaths and let them go. Sometimes I still struggle with the need for my addiction. The drinks and pills filled a void in me, and after all this time, I realize how lucky I am to have beat them, even though it's a struggle. But I finally have come to terms with how much I have to lose if I had continued using the drinks and pills. Or God forbid went to something even worse.

Opening my eyes, looking at the sky that looks awe-inspiring tonight, I do something I don't do enough. "God, I know you don't hear from me too often, but just wanted to let you know that no matter what you have planned for me for the rest of my life, I can never thank you enough for allowing my Fern to come home. I'm not gonna promise you all kinds of stuff. I just want it out there that I realize the gift you are giving me and I will treasure it until eternity."

Spending a couple of minutes just gazing at the

beauty before me, I finish my beer and go to stand when a shooting star goes flying by, right in my view. I don't believe in a lot, but on this night watching that star I truly know it was my answer from a higher power, letting me know that my words were heard.

CHAPTER THIRTY

PRESENT ~ MY SUGAR IS HOME ~

(Gabriel)

Waking on Saturday morning, I am overcome with my emotions. Realizing that finally this is the last time I sleep alone in our bed brings me almost to tears. Damn, I hope I can hold it together today in front of Fern. Don't want her to think I've gotten soft in her absence.

With my hands behind my head, I take some time to just be. Never one to let folks know what I'm feeling, today it's going to be hard to keep my emotions under control. It's a great day with my sugar coming home, but the emotional aspect has been playing with my head for the last couple of days. As happy as I am that Fern has made it, and the stem cell transplant has taken, and she is getting stronger each and every day, there are no guarantees. My mind drifts to Lydia and I shiver, knowing that could have easily been Fern. Those poor babies of hers will never know their momma. Right then I make a promise that we will raise them the way Lydia would be proud of and we will keep her memory alive.

Trinity has been wonderful with Charlie and Emma. There are photos of Lydia and her babies all over their rooms here, at the cabin, and even at Trinity and Cadence's home. Her presence is felt everywhere.

I'm just about to get out of bed and start my day, when I hear the doorbell. Really? Who the hell is here, today of all days? I explained to them the entire plan so obviously someone didn't listen.

Grabbing my jeans, pulling them up as I walk to the door, I look to see who it is and a smile hits my face. But of course, should have seen this comin'.

Opening the door wide, I squint as the sun hits me in the eyes.

"Look what the dog dragged in. What are y'all doing here?"

Des, Wolf, and Cadence stare back at me with shit-eating grins on their faces.

"Doc, you had to expect to see us sometime today," Cadence bellows out.

"I'm here to make sure these two don't aggravate you before Fern comes home," Wolf states as he walks past me into the house.

Des is watching all the interaction and after Cadence follows Wolf into the kitchen looking for coffee, I glance at my best friend, boss, and confidant. He sees me watching him so he heads my way, stopping directly in front of me. Reaching for me, he pulls me into a man hug, pounding on my back. "Gabriel..."

My head shoots up because I can count on one hand how many times he has called me by my given name.

"Before this day gets started, I want to share with you that not since my parents were killed have I wished, prayed, and bargained for someone to pull through. Since Fern got ill, I've done just that. You know I'm not a religious guy, but both Dee Dee and I have been to church praying for a *'happily ever after'* for you and Fern. Today I'm here, brother, to tell you how happy I am for the outcome of this battle. You, Doc, aren't only my best friend but also a man I have admired for many years. Do me a favor, never take it for granted because as we know life changes on a dime."

Shock that badass alpha Des is showing his emotions, has me overwhelmed and trying to keep it together.

"Des, thanks so much. We can never repay you for all you have done but know this—it comes from here." As I pound my chest. "If I could have the choice to pick a brother, he would have been you. In fact, for all intents and purposes, you are my brother."

Just as we're going to finish, I hear from behind me, "All right, do ya need some more time so you can bond? 'Cause from here all I see are two middle-aged men getting all mushy. Damn, why the hell did ya hit me in the head, Wolf, for fuck's sake?"

Turning we see Cadence holding his head as Wolf is grinning behind him. We all start to laugh as Wolf looks our way.

"Put some coffee on. Got time to just sit and have coffee, Doc?"

"Yeah, I do, Wolf."

As we all head to the kitchen, I realize again how fucking lucky, no blessed, I am to have these people in my life.

Seeing how nervous Fern is as we drive toward our house, I grab her hand, giving it a squeeze.

"Sugar, it will be okay. Promise, it's just us, so no expectations. One day at a time is our new motto, got it?"

She nods, looking lost as she watches the streets go by. The closer we get to home, the more anxious she appears. Damn, I wonder if Dr. Davids should've given her something for anxiety.

"Sugar, did you take all your meds today?"

Her head shoots up. "No, crap. I didn't take the anxiety pill. Probably why I feel like I'm crawling out of my own skin. Why, Gabriel, am I so nervous? It's my home and you're my husband. Doesn't make any sense to me."

"Fern, remember what Julie told us? Each new thing will affect you differently. Don't fight it. Let it out. We'll talk about it and move on. Sugar, we're past the hardest part, now it's the final run. As long as we keep the lines of communication open, we're good."

I make the left turn onto our road as Fern leans forward, looking toward our house.

We have done a lot to the house inside and outside, so glancing at her shocked look I can understand why she is so surprised. All the damaged cedar siding was replaced, along with the roof. The front and back porch have been repaired, not to mention the landscaping has been gone over. Pulling in the drive, she sees the first sign hanging from the garage.

"WELCOME HOME, FERN. WE LOVE YOU!"

Immediately she starts crying.

Putting the car in park, I unbuckle my seat belt as she does hers and I pull her to me.

"Sugar, come on now, this is the happiest day of my life besides the day you said 'I do.' No tears. Don't want you to get upset."

"These are happy tears, Gabriel. The love I feel fills my heart. How did we ever get so lucky to have these people in our lives?"

Holding her for a few seconds, I gently place her back in her seat, telling her to wait. I will help her out. Walking around the front of the truck, I notice the one vehicle parked in the street. Well, I kind of knew they would be here for Fern. Opening her door, I help her out and we walk to the front of our house. She is taking everything in so I give her time.

When I get to the front door, it opens before I can put my key in. Looking up, I see Cadence, Trinity, and Baby Hope with huge smiles on their faces. Fern looks up, squeals, and moves quickly to Trinity as they fall into each other, laughing and crying at the same time. Cadence reaches over grabbing Hope, handing her to me. I look down at my 'granddaughter' who is looking right back at me smiling. At this moment there isn't anything else I want in my life. It is perfect.

Entering the house, the aroma of something hits me and I realize how hungry I am.

"Damn, something smells good. You guys have been busy."

Trinity looks over Fern's shoulder smiling. "It's baked chicken and all the fixings. Thought that would be good and gentle on Mom's stomach, being her first day home."

Looking at the young woman holding my wife in her arms, calling her mom, makes me realize how lucky we are to have Trinity in our lives. She was a blessing to Cadence and without all the research she did, Fern might not be here today.

Winking at Trinity, which brings a sparkle to her eyes, I reply back to her.

"So dinner is just for Fern. Do the rest of us just get to watch or is there enough for all of us?"

Pulling away from each other, Trinity approaches me tentatively. "Dad, you know if we do something for Mom it's automatically including you too. I love you both equally and with my whole heart. You mean more to me than my own parents ever could. I know you're much younger than them but to me it feels right to call you Dad and Mom. Not all the time but at the times that mean the most.

Grabbing her with my one free hand, I pull her to me as Hope looks down, giggling at her mother. Minutes go by as Trinity and I share our moment. Realizing it has gotten quiet, I look to see Fern in Cadence's arms softly crying as he holds her tight to him. He is whispering in her ear as she struggles to control her emotions. As she caresses his cheek, Cadence moves into her hand. Finally, Fern clears her throat, wipes her eyes then moves her eyes to Trinity.

"I'm starved. Let's eat."

CHAPTER THIRTY-ONE

PRESENT ~ FAMILY IS FAMILY ~

(Gabriel)

"You aren't upset we were here are you, Doc? Both Trinity and I talked about it, and Fern is so special to both of us we felt that we needed to be here, so if we stepped on your toes, don't be too upset."

Watching him talk I can't believe how far Cadence has come. Damn, just a few years ago he was a manwhore and now he is a husband, father, and one hell of a man.

"Cadence, I'm not upset. I'm actually glad you were here. Fern was really feeling out of sorts and having some normalcy made the transition into the house easier for her. We still have a road to battle and each day something else will come up, but we talked about it and are going to take it one day at a time."

We sit on the couch catching up as Trinity, Fern, and Baby Hope sit at the dining room table talking. I catch Fern's eye and wink her way, which brings a smile to her face and a surprising blush to her cheeks. I keep an eye on her and see her looking my way more and more. Feeling like our lives are getting back to *normal,* I catch up with Cadence.

As time goes by and the evening approaches, I see my wife struggling to stay awake. Just as I'm about to say something, Cadence beats me to it.

"Trin, time to pack up our shit. Mom's tired. She needs her rest. Let's clean this up before we go." He walks to the kitchen and starts loading the dishwasher as both Fern and I watch in shock. Cadence at one time lived with us and to say he was a bit of a pig when he was here is an understatement. Well, times are changing, apparently.

"Cadence, leave it. We can do that after you go. Please, you have done enough," Fern states softly, followed by a yawn.

"Mom, he's right. Let us do a quick cleanup and we'll be out of your hair. You don't need to start right away first day home cleaning and stuff."

"Can I hold Hope while you clean up?"

Just as I'm about to tell my wife no because of the issue with the baby and germs, Trinity goes to the diaper bag pulling out a baby mask and wipes. Walking to the high chair, she cleans Hope's hands and puts the mask on her, lifting her up and giving her to Fern, who is giggling.

"Hope, honey, look at you. Mommy's put a mask on you. She's so silly."

Watching the kids in the kitchen and Fern playing

with Hope, I sit back and just take it in. This is what life is truly about. Not fame and fortune, but family and we all have a different definition on family. Neither Cadence nor Trinity are blood relatives, but they mean more to me than my own family. They've been there for both of us throughout the last months that Fern has been fighting her cancer. Not to mention, if not for Trinity's research we wouldn't have gotten this far.

Cadence comes over and plops down next to me smiling. He just sits there staring at me with that look on his face. Finally, I just give in.

"What're you smiling about?"

Looking like he is thinking for a minute while rubbing his hand through his hair, his head shoots up as he glances my way.

"I just feel so full of happiness to see her home. More importantly that she's healthy. She is healthy, right? Doc, I was never so scared in my life. Especially..." He lowers his voice looking behind me before continuing, "When we lost Lydia I kind of freaked out, knowing it could happen just as easily to Fern. If it wasn't for Trinity, I don't know what I would have done. She's my anchor, always there to make sure I'm okay without any judgment."

"Yeah, not sure how you got so lucky with that one. But remember you guys had some bumps in the road in the beginning so you could have walked, but you stuck it out and I'm proud of you, Cadence. It feels like finally everyone in the Horde family is getting what they've always wanted. Can't ask for more, can we?"

As we sit and talk, I keep an eye on Fern as Trinity changes Hope and puts on the little onesie pj's. Fern is just standing, watching the process with a look of awe in her face. God, she would have made a wonderful mother. The one thing she wanted above everything else and I couldn't give it to her. Fuck. Talk about a mood spoiler.

"Doc, if you're thinking what I think you are, it's not your fault. You both would have been good parents. And things worked themselves out. Remember, when they can come over, you'll have Charlie and Emma here and believe me, Mom will become their second mommy. She will do right by Lydia, as we all know."

Listening to his words something comes to mind.

"Cadence, why all of a sudden are you and Trinity calling Fern Mom? No, she loves it and I think it's awesome, but what changed?"

"Doc that's all Trinity. She watched Fern fading and tried to think of a way to let Mom know how much we love her. One night we were talking and she said that it felt like she was losing her mom. That the closest she has ever come to a mother was Fern. She was like a second mom. It hit Trin at that moment and the next time we visited she told that to Fern and called her Mom for the first time. I just think it lets Fern/Mom know how much I care for her, even though my mom lives here now too. They both get it."

After the kids leave, we sit on the sofa cuddled next to each other with the TV on, but neither of us are watching it. Background noise. I feel like that weight in my chest is finally gone. I glance down to see Fern looking up at me hesitantly.

"Sugar, what's going on in that mind of yours?"

"I finally feel like I'm home. I have to say that the work everyone did here is breathtaking. Can't believe it's our home. I'm trying to take it all in, but truthfully, Gabriel, it's so overwhelming to me. I left here so sick and the house was in such need of repair and I get back here healthy and the house has had a facelift. It will take me some time to take in everything. Our bathroom, I could and probably will, get lost in it. A claw-foot tub? Really, husband? You know that has always been a dream of mine."

"I know, sugar, and it is big enough for two, just sayin'."

She drops her head as once again I see a blush come up her neck, covering her cheeks.

Reaching over, I lift her head and look into her eyes. "Fern, I know you need time and we've all the time in the world, but you know me better than anyone else and I'm gonna speak my mind. Won't step over any boundaries you set, but I'm not gonna just ignore how breathtaking you are and how much I want to be with you, however that ends up to be. Sex isn't the only way we can be intimate. Sitting here with you in my arms is better than anything at the moment. So don't panic when I say shit...ouch, what did you pinch me for?"

"Gabriel, mouth. I know you have been swearing up a storm, but I'm home now so please let's try to get back to normal," she says with a cute half smile.

Damn, it's so good to have her in my arms, pinching me for swearing in our home. Can't ask for anything more.

CHAPTER THIRTY-TWO

PRESENT ~ TIME WAITS FOR NO ONE ~

(Fern)

I pull out the kitchen chair and drop into it. Gosh, I'm totally out of shape. Looking around there is food in aluminum trays covered with foil or Saran wrap. It has taken me all of the morning and most of the afternoon to get to this point. Tomorrow is the christening for Hope and I offered to help Trinity by making some of the salads for the party. They're going all out. Since they live above the garage of Wheels & Hogs in an awesome apartment with that huge parking lot, Cadence came up with the idea to rent a tent for the party. I told both of them they could have the party here, but since I was just recently released and still on some restrictions, Cadence thanked me, but said they had a plan. So, I am on salad duty.

Taking a much-needed break, I sip my tea and reflect on the last month. Man, it's so true time never stops. Thinking about what has happened since I got home, my mind is overwrought with everything I have accomplished.

First, once settled Gabriel and I started to go to therapy to talk about my feelings toward our sex life. My counselor, Joan, is really something. After just the first visit she gave us homework and after each visit we get an assignment. The homework is to bring us closer and make me more comfortable with the physical side of our marriage.

Now I never knew what *The Kama Sutra* was until Joan recommended we get this book. Gabriel went after work one night and little did either of us know it was more of a picture book then a reading book. When he handed me the book, Gabriel couldn't even look me in the eyes but had a huge grin on his face. Even now I blush just thinking about opening that book. Dang, at first, I thought Gabriel was playing with me until I took the time and not only looked at the pictures but also read some of the information regarding how spiritual sex can be. And it isn't all about the act itself, the intercourse isn't what they refer to as sex.

Now we haven't had sex yet, but there are some of those positions I truly love. *The Close Up* especially and *The Amazon* is also a good one we do sometimes in our underwear. Silly, but that little bit of material makes me feel safe. Now *The Bridge* made both Gabriel and I break out hysterically. To think of Gabriel doing a backbend and me sitting on his penis bouncing up and down made even me laugh. Not ever happening, even Gabriel gave that one thumbs-down.

We have started from fresh as my husband keeps telling me. We have been on numerous dates; he even brought me home a bouquet of flowers. Silk of course, but they're gorgeous and they now have a home on the table in the screen porch. I feel closer to Gabriel, now more than ever. He found this interview with the singer Sting that had him explaining how to increase sensual closeness. In the beginning I was uncomfortable, but Gabriel is persistent and patient. We've tried different things, and at first it was just me taking care of his needs, but I don't know what's happening to me. The longer I am home, and with Gabriel all the time, I'm starting to see what attracted me to him physically in the first place. I mean looking at him he takes my breath away, but at the same time I get all warm and tingly. I feel like a schoolgirl and when I explain these confusing feelings to Joan, she just smiles and tells me that what is happening is normal. Joan also went as far as to guide me not to put boundaries on our relationship. She said to go with the flow, so that is what I am trying to do.

Sipping my tea, I bring up what happened the other day. Coming out of the shower, Gabriel walked in, not thinking, and I was so shocked I also stood there completely naked. The look in my husband's eyes had me all tingly and at the same time very uncomfortable. He had not seen me totally naked since before my transplant. Now between all the different things either in me or attached to me during surgery and after, I have new scars all over. Also just from being bedridden for so long I have lost muscle tone and weight. I've never been a real curvy woman, but now I feel sickly. As Gabriel took in my body slowly, my breath stuck in my throat. When his eyes reached mine, he must have seen my trepidation as he immediately went into the bedroom, grabbed his robe, and came toward me, helping me into it then pulled me to his chest. His words filled my heart and soul.

"Sugar, damn woman, I won't be able to close my eyes without seeing your beautiful body." As I tried interrupting him, Gabriel put his index finger to my lips. "Fern, do you know what I see when I look at you? I see a slip of a woman who can conquer anything that comes her way with quiet dignity and firm determination. A woman who loves her family with her whole heart and even when insecurities threaten to break her, she fights to overcome them and she just lives her life. I'm so proud of you, sugar."

From that moment on something changed in me. Not sure what, but I watched Gabriel more, wanted to be near him always, and now crave his touch. Not always in a sexual way, but I just need his hands on me. So that's what we do now. We talk about everything and all my feelings. Gabriel gives me everything I need and sometimes a bit more because he pushes my limits. He's holding back because of my recovery, but that part of him is never far from making an appearance.

Break over, I go about finishing my salads and clean up the kitchen. Once done and all are placed in the fridge, I head to our bedroom, take a shower, and cover up with Gabriel's robe. Exhausted beyond belief, I lie on our bed with the intention to take a short nap. Well, at least I have good intentions, too bad my body isn't listening.

Feeling warmth across my entire backside, I struggle to open my eyes. Disoriented for a minute or two, I just enjoy the heat covering me. That's until I feel something hard pressing up against my butt cheeks. I immediately try to move away from what I'm assuming is Gabriel's hard-on. His hand across my belly holds me firm as he adjusts himself so the hard length of him isn't touching me any longer. Part of me is happy but there is another part that didn't want him to move away. That part of me wants the old Gabriel back, the one who takes control while I just submit. That was so much easier than all of this tension, worry, and nervousness around my husband.

"Sugar, did you sleep well? I didn't mean to wake you, but didn't want to throw your sleep pattern off. I stopped and picked up some chicken and that movie you wanted to see. You know the one, *Fifty Shades of Grey*. So it's chick flick night."

I can hear the laughter in his voice. Damn him. He knew how curious I was about that movie. Lydia and I both read the books, and man, did we have some conversations. Just thinking about her brings heaviness to my heart. Gabriel catches it immediately.

"Fern, honey, what is it? Sugar, we don't have to watch that movie if it's going to upset you or you can watch it alone."

"No, Gabriel, I was just thinking on the conversations Lydia and I had over those three books. There was stuff in there neither of us had any idea what it was and had to look it up. We spent hours talking and laughing about it and how we would watch the movie together when it came out and we were granted our freedom. Damn, Gabriel, it hurts so badly. Why didn't she make and I did? That haunts me so much."

Pulling me closer to him, his mouth by my ear, I can feel each and every breath he takes.

"Fern, maybe it's time to talk to Joan about Lydia. And before you get all bratty, I mean really share all the feelings you are working through. If anyone can help you, it's her."

"You're right, honey, I need to work on this. I feel so many things when it comes to Lydia, but I need to be strong because eventually Charlie and Emma will be spending a lot of time with us. Please have patience with me. I'm trying so hard to be the best me possible."

He turns me toward him, lifting my face then giving me a soft kiss.

"Sugar, we have all the time in the world. There are no time restraints and I know you're missing your friend. Grief is something hard to get through. Just know I'm here for you and will do my best to always have your back, honey."

Caressing his face, feeling the stubble on his cheeks, I surprise the hell out of him when I reach up, pulling him to me, and kiss him. I meant it to be only a kiss, but something was pushing me on and I pressed for more.

Tentatively, I brush my tongue over his fuller lower lip as he growls. Putting pressure on his lip with my tongue, he opens and our tongues press together. It's a softer, gentler French kiss, but still I feel something deep in my belly that I haven't felt in a really long time.

Gabriel's hold gets tighter and the noises coming from him give me the push I need. Moving my body, I lie over part of him and take the kiss to the next level. Just when I'm going to pull back, Gabriel takes over, and man, that's what I want so badly.

He takes my mouth like a desperate man and it makes me feel so wanted and loved. His hands go up and down my body, never touching anywhere for too long, but his hands brush my breasts then put pressure between my legs briefly. Getting more into it, I grab his butt and pull him closer to my body. Just as I'm ready to jump off the cliff and go for it, Gabriel lifts his head, caressing my face with his hands.

"Sugar, how you doing?" Looking into those emerald-green eyes that I love so much kind of speechless, I just nod.

"Fern, I need you to tell me you're okay. You know what I need, sugar."

"I'm good. No, better than good, Gabriel. I feel

well, I mean, I feel, you know, umm, tingling down there."

His eyes darken, as his breath gets shorter. Watching me for a minute or two he finally asks, "What is it that you want, sugar? Tell me what you need from me."

Watching his mouth move, I lean in my mouth by his ear and whisper, "You, Gabriel. I want you."

Immediately, I'm on my back with his body pressing down on mine, while his mouth takes mine in a possessive, hungry kiss. His hands caress the fullness of my breasts gently at first, and then as he continues to watch me, he starts to really massage deeply into them, pushing up from underneath, making the blood go to my nipples, then tweaking them. The feeling is so, gosh, I don't even have words for it. I feel needy for the first time in forever. Feeling his fingers pinching each nipple, then stretching them, my memories kick in thinking of the times I wore his nipple clamps. Just the thought has my nipples hardening until they start to actually hurt sweetly.

His hands travel down my waist, caressing my softer tummy, reaching down to the hot spot between my legs. Ever so slowly his fingers massage my inner thighs then go back up to my hip bones, rubbing and caressing, always getting close to where I need him, but never touching. I am slowly going out of my mind. I feel like I'm on fire as my clit throbs constantly.

Gabriel keeps getting closer and closer to that bundle of nerves, but still hasn't touched it. I notice that even though I feel like I'm burning up, there is no moisture touching his fingers. Immediately self-conscious, I try to pull back, but as always, he's watching me. Kissing the swell of my breasts, he reaches to the nightstand, pulling the top drawer out, moving stuff around, coming out with a magenta bottle. Guessing it is some type of lube, I feel sick to my stomach. Never in all the years we have been together has he needed to use anything. We would actually joke about how wet I became from his touch. My mood starts to fade and I push my body farther into the bed and away from his hand. Just as quickly, he pulls me back, growling my name.

"Fern, don't do that. There's nothing that happens in this bed that we shy away from. We knew this could happen and I am prepared, sugar. Not a thing to be embarrassed about. Give this," he motions between us, "a chance."

CHAPTER THIRTY-THREE

PRESENT ~ SEXUAL TENSION ~

(Gabriel)

Watching her struggle with her body letting her down, I give her time to adjust. I'm not going to stop when she finally has given me the green light. I've been waiting for this moment for way too long.

Shaking the bottle, I pop the top, letting some of the liquid into the palm of my hand. Instantly my hand feels warm and tingling. Yeah, this is gonna work just fine.

Reaching down, I lightly tap Fern's clit with fingers coated in this sensation lubrication. I watch her closely as it starts to work and I know this as her legs scissor open and close to relieve the pressure it's putting on that button of nerves.

She sucks in her bottom lip, nibbling it back and forth, watching me watch her. Her hands fisted into the comforter on the bed, I start to rub that special spot and a sigh escapes her lips. She relaxes back into the bed, body seeming to float on clouds.

"Sugar, how does that feel? Does it help or is it bothersome?'

"No, Gabriel, doesn't bother me. Please don't stop. I think I need more."

Smiling to myself as I gaze at her face, which is flushed with need, as her little body wiggles on the bed grasping for her release impatiently waiting to see what I do next. I lean forward and blow my hot breath on her swollen clit. The moan that escapes her lips is music to my ears. I repeat the action until she is squirming on the bed. Running my finger lightly over the lubrication, I gently push part of my finger into her center. Her back arches as she pushes her shoulders into the bed, spreading her legs at the same time. God, she's fucking beautiful. I work my finger in and out of her, giving her body time to adjust. When I finally have my entire finger inside, I wait a moment, then reach forward with my fingertip, rubbing it over the roughened nerve ending deep inside. Fern squeals and closes her eyes tightly. Nope, not happening, I want that orgasm.

"Fern, open your eyes. I want to watch you fall apart."

As her eyes pop open, I begin pumping my finger in and out until her body relaxes a bit and I can fit two fingers inside of her. The sighs and moans escaping her mouth are driving me insane, but tonight is all about Fern recapturing her sexual power. So going slower than I usually do, I play her body like a violin. She is twitching and turning to try and get the pressure exactly where she needs it. I'm waiting for her to tell me what she needs. It takes a couple of more intense minutes until she screams

"Gabriel, please...oh God, please make me come. I'm burning up from the inside out. Please...oh God, right there. Yes!

Feeling her body clench around my fingers tight inside of her, refusing to release me, I continue to pump in and out until she lets everything go. Slowing the motion down until she is spent. I finally pull them out, bringing them to my mouth. She watches me as I lick them clean.

"Goddamn, sugar I have missed that unique taste that is only you. How are you feeling?"

She stretches and curves her body into mine. "I feel really relaxed and tired, husband. So tired, but also so peaceful. That was...I just don't have words."

Looking down at her smiling up at me fills my heart.

"Thank you, Gabriel, for not letting me get in my head. Man, my body is humming. Can't remember the last time I had an orgasm. So tired," she finishes on a yawn.

"Go to sleep, sugar. I'll be back in a bit. Know I love you, Fern. Always have and always will. Close your eyes, sugar."

"But what about you, Gabriel? You need release

too. I could do something." Finishing, Fern tries to hide another yawn.

"Not to worry. We have the rest of our lives to take care of each other. Sleep, Fern."

As I go to leave the room, she snuggles into our bed. I am sure in less than five minutes she'll be in a deep relaxed sleep.

When I return back to our bed, pulling Fern close, this is the first night she sleeps completely through the entire night peacefully.

It has been a few weeks since that night Fern finally let me back in. Her reaction and orgasm have been streaming through my mind ever since. I've been walking around with a hard-on constantly. The next morning I could see the difference in her. She was more confident and self-assured. That was the final step for us to get back to our normal lives. No, we didn't have intercourse, but being able to touch my wife so intimately and make her feel how much I love her was to me better than having sex. That will come. It's just a matter of time.

"Hey, Doc. Daydreaming again?"

Hearing Des yell across the garage, I realize once again I slipped away from my daily grind. Grinning like an idiot, I nod my head.

"Yeah, guess so, Des. You know how it is when you get something stuck in your head and can't get it out."

"Glad to see it's something that puts that smile back on your face, brother. Been a while since we've seen it."

As we bullshit back and forth, I realize that I have come full circle since Fern has come home. Life is good and I'm so fucking happy I can't stop grinning.

"So what has you so pumped up, Doc? I take it Fern is feeling well and things are going good between you both, now that she's home?"

"Definitely, Des, things are great. Each day reminds me of how far we have come and how much we have to be thankful for. Ann called and Charlie and Emma are gonna spend the weekend with us so I can simply say I'm a fucking lucky man."

"Is Fern happy the kiddos are coming by? She ready for that, 'cause I will tell you; they're a handful. Ran Dee Dee and my asses off when they were by us. I loved having them, but when Trinity came to get them, I was one tired son of a bitch. Dee too."

Nodding at him, I understand his underlying question. "Fern has spoken to both her physician and therapist and they each agree she needs to keep pushing forward and they have told her she is ready. I know she's nervous and afraid, one they won't know her or like her, and two, think she is trying to replace Lydia, which we all know is not her intention. Lydia knew how badly Fern wanted a family and that courageous woman made sure Fern would have one, even if it was at her own expense. I admire the shit out of her and wish she could have beat the damn cancer."

As I get back to work trying to keep my mind on the

job at hand, thinking that this weekend will either be one of the best yet or a total bust, and it all depends on two little kids and the love of my life.

Watching Fern and Emma playing with the baby dolls, my heart is just so full of love. Fern's face is flushed, she's giggling and laughing with the little girl as they interact, playing mommies to the plastic baby dolls. Emma is at that age that she is cute as a button with the Minnie Mouse little voice.

Just as I'm about to sit back and relax for a minute, a body lands on my midsection, taking my breath away.

"Gabriel, let's wrestle. Can you teach me some moves?"

I try to catch the wiggling boy, but he is as elusive as ever. "Charlie, sit still, kiddo. No wrestling, too close to bedtime. How about I tell you a story and then maybe if you're good we can have some ice cream before bed. Sound like a plan?"

"Yes, yes I want ice cream."

"Okay, story first, then ice cream, but ya got to sit still and listen."

Nodding, he crawls off my lap and cuddles right into my side, knees up over my legs, arm around my waist. This just feels so right and thinking that we're able to enjoy this because of Lydia, in my mind I take a moment to thank the most selfless person I have ever met. In her death she enabled the four of us to be this unique family unit, and I'll never forget her or take any of this for granted ever.

CHAPTER THIRTY-FOUR

PAST & PRESENT ~ LOVE IS IN THE AIR ~

(Fern)

I was constantly having flashbacks of that first night Gabriel and I made love. Thinking back on all the planning he went through to make my first time unforgettable. As days turn into weeks, my body has come full circle. Where once sex wasn't something I gave much thought to since my cancer diagnosis, now it's on my mind quiet frequently. Especially while watching Gabriel and Charlie in the backyard doing the usual weekend yardwork. Charlie has taken to my husband like I can't believe, but it makes sense really. Charlie hasn't really had a father or a male figure in his life. Those two are inseparable, which brings joy to my heart.

Now Emma and I are working on our relationship too, but it's different. Charlie had a mommy he remembers, Lydia, and being older than Emma he's struggling with the loss of the most important person in his life, as Emma's memories are vague. We're working through that and building on our own relationship. Even though she's young, I don't ever want Emma to think I'm trying to replace Lydia, as that is not my intention.

Bringing my attention back to our yard, my heart rate rapidly increases watching Gabriel without his shirt on and those low riding jeans of his. My breath catches, looking at my husband of almost sixteen years. Gosh, our lives have been through so much.

I think to myself how lucky I am that Gabriel is my husband, because most men wouldn't put up with all of my health issues and the total lack of sex. The other day when walking in the bathroom to put towels away, I was shocked to find Gabriel in there masturbating. As his eyes met mine, he never stopped, and surprising myself, I actually watched and I even got a bit horny. Afterward, we sat on our bed and he explained that he would never pressure me for anything, but since I came home, he was doing that regularly because as he put it "You make me horny, sugar." I told my husband that since I was home when he feels the need, he should come to me. I'd love to touch him. At my words, he laughed.

"Fern, you mean you'll jerk me off when the need arises?"

We both laughed at that moment.

After speaking with Joan, she explained that time does heal everything. My lack of sexual feeling is due to multiple things, including my lack of self-confidence, so we're working on that in my therapy sessions. She has had me work on my appearance, hence the visit with the girls to the salon. Dee Dee and I have gone on a couple of shopping dates to bring my clothes to this decade. Giggling, I will never forget her face when she looked in my closet. That was so much fun picking out new and vibrant colored clothing.

Hearing Gabriel's deep, virile laugh, my head jerks to the window again. He's chasing Charlie around the yard, giving the young boy head starts, acting like he can't catch the boy. They both have red faces from the running and the heat, while laughing continuously at each other's antics.

With the sun shining into his wavy auburn hair, which he is wearing a bit longer nowadays, his emerald-green eyes sparkling, part of me wishes I could go out there, grab him into my arms and have a day spent in bed. Suddenly shocked at my thoughts, I feel the warmth between my legs and the need running through my veins. Damn, I want Gabriel right now. The more I think on this, the more turned on I become. My breasts seem to swell within my bra and I can feel my nipples harden, feeling taut with need. Finally feeling like a woman, I just sit back and enjoy this almost forgotten feeling of want and need.

As I stand and walk to the window once again, something catches Gabriel's eyes and he looks my way. Somehow, he sees something because his eyes flare suddenly with need and he seems to stand taller and broader. Then that shit-eating grin of his appears as he gives me a small wave. I wave back and pull myself together so I can go play with Emma.

Later that night after both Emma and Charlie have fallen into their beds, exhausted after dinner, baths, and a story, I head back to the family room to find Gabriel stretched out on the couch watching a sporting event. Which kind, I don't really know or care. I am totally wiped so I head to the kitchen for something to drink.

"Hey, Gabriel, you want anything while I'm out here?"

"Yeah, sugar, if you don't mind, a beer please."

Grabbing a beer for him and a bottle of flavored water for me, I turn out the light and head toward him as he reaches out for the bottle.

"Thanks, Fern. I appreciate it. Not sure about you, but damn that little boy wore me out. Could fall asleep right here."

Smiling at him, I nod. "I understand you perfectly. Emma has way too much energy and imagination. Probably going to take some time, but I don't think I'll ever keep up with her, but am loving every moment with them, aren't you? Lydia left us two precious gifts, Gabriel."

"Yeah, she did and I'm thankful every day, Fern. I couldn't love those kids more if they were our biological children. Hey, don't mean to change the subject, but I need to know. What was that look from you for earlier when I was playing with Charlie?"

Blushing and trying to avoid eye contact, I ignore him at first. But being Gabriel, he pushes.

"Come on, sugar, tell me what was going through your mind at that moment. It has been driving me crazy all day."

Looking directly into his eyes I let it out. "Gabriel, I was watching you half naked in the yard with Charlie and it brought back many memories. It also made me horny to see... hey...ummm"

That is all I get out because he reaches over, pulling me on top of his body, and devouring my mouth. His hands run up and down my body as he pushes his hips up so I can feel his hard, long length between my legs. Moaning, I reach my hands around his waist, pulling him closer to me. All of a sudden, I can't keep my hands off of his body. Reaching under his T-shirt, I push my hands up and then down over his nipples, lightly running my nails over them, making him growl. I have so missed that sexy as hell growl. As we continue to touch, squeeze, raising the heat level, bumping and grinding on each other, getting closer and closer to each other. The temperature seems to skyrocket in the room as I realize that the time has come for me to show my husband how much I want him. How much I love him.

CHAPTER THIRTY-FIVE

PRESENT ~ WHOLE AGAIN ~

(Fern)

Pushing Gabriel away from me, I hear the very faint moan coming from him. I smile knowing he's thinking I'm slowing this down. Little does he know how lucky he is going to get tonight. Glancing up into his confused eyes, I push a bit more on his massive chest as I gaze lovingly at him.

"Gabriel, get off of me. Honey, I want to go to our bedroom now. Please!"

Jumping off of me, he pulls me off the couch and down the small hallway to our bedroom. No stopping or passing go. As we enter, I turn, closing and locking the bedroom door in case one of the children wakes up. They don't need a visual.

As I reach for him, he gently pushes me to the edge of the bed, kneeling in front of me. "Fern, honey, you sure? Sugar, if I start, it's going to be next to impossible to stop 'cause I want you so much. Don't want to pressure you, but I have to ask."

I place my fingers over his lips, shaking my head in acknowledgment. "Gabriel, I have never been surer of anything in my life. Please make love to me."

Watching the emotions crossing his face, I finally grasp the depth of his love for me. I see it in his emerald-green eyes as he watches me watch him.

Reaching, I grasp his face between my hands and join our lips in an emotion-filled kiss, hoping all the feelings I am putting into the kiss he can feel.

"Gabriel, I want to please you so much, but it has been so long. Please help me, show me what you want."

"Sugar, all I want, all I have ever wanted, is you, just you. Come here."

As we fall into each other's arms, I feel like I'm finally home. Home in my Gabriel's arms, feeling his desire pressing into my body as his arms wrap around me, holding me close to him as our hearts beat as one. I can finally take the next steps so Gabriel and I are once again together in every way two people can be who love each other.

(Gabriel)

Watching Fern slowly letting her guard down, I know tonight is the night I'll get my wife and lover back. My hands itch to feel her body as my mouth waters to taste her uniqueness. Watching her for signals, one way or another, I reach over, taking my time. I first remove her blouse, then her slacks. Looking at her in her plain bra and undies, suddenly it hits me that Fern could be in a burlap sack and she would still be sexy to me.

Looking at how her breasts fill the cups of her bra; I'm craving her rosy nipples. I want to nibble and suck them until she screams my name. My eyes travel down her soft belly as she shifts from one foot to the other. Bringing my eyes to hers, I lose my breath as I see her eyes are filled with desire. Desire for me.

"Sugar, last time. You sure?" At her head nod, I growl. "Words, Fern. I need your words."

"Yes, Gabriel, I am sure. I need to feel you."

Losing the little bit of control I have left, I reach for her, lifting her in my arms as I walk to the side of the bed. Gently placing her in the middle of the bed, I take off my T-shirt and jeans as her eyes never leave my body. She watches every move I make, licking her lips as if she can't wait to get them on me. My cock is hard as a brick, throbbing and quite painful, but to me that is the best feeling. Grabbing ahold of my length, I run my hand up then down the length then adjust as her eyes widen at my actions.

"Fern, look at me. Sugar, look at me. Tell me what you want right now."

"I want your body on mine, in mine, all around mine. Please, Gabriel."

Lying next to her, I grab her, pulling her close as

my mouth connects with hers. She tastes like vanilla as I eat at her lips, pulling and nipping them into my mouth. As I run my tongue down her fuller lower lip, she hesitantly opens up, allowing me entry. My tongue runs up and down the length of hers as we reacquaint ourselves with each other. I love the feel of her warmth in my mouth and on my skin as her small hands start to roam the planes of my body. As we continue to kiss, I hold her head in place to get that angle I love that gives me unlimited access to her. She relaxes into my hold, moaning into my mouth as my heartbeat takes off. Trying to hold back my passion, as all I want is to drive into her warmth and feel her tighten around me, welcoming me home, I continue to kiss, nibble, and heat up Fern's body, preparing hers to take mine.

Time has no meaning to us and it could have been five minutes or fifty, we don't know. We are so in tune to each other that when I reach for the clasp of her bra, Fern beats me to it and unclasps it, allowing it to fall from her shoulders. Watching the soft flesh reveal itself, I feel my cock jump in my briefs. Damn, feeling the precum as my cock rubs up and down the material, I try to hold myself back so this doesn't end way too soon and I embarrass myself.

Rediscovering Fern is so much more fun than I could have imagined. She has changed not only physically, but also emotionally. I discover a new woman in Fern, including new tickle spots that make her giggle and some sensitive areas that make her tremble and moan. I take my time to find them all.

Moaning, sighing, and crying out, Fern makes me want her more and more, which makes me harder and hotter with each sound.

Placing her hands on our headboard, wrapping her hands around the wood, she holds on tightly.

"Sugar, keep your hands here. Don't move them unless I tell you."

I stare at her face, hands on both sides, caressing her cheeks, running my fingers over her lips and pushing one finger into her mouth. Shocked, she starts to suck on my finger, making my dick throb with need. As I watch, she continues to suck my finger as if it was my cock. Running her tongue along my finger joint, I really want to shove her down on my cock it feels so good. Pulling free, I bring both hands to her breasts, massaging and squeezing, watching her face closely. As her eyes begin to shut, I start to pull and tug on those rosy nipples. Lightly at first, I nibble on one then the other as she starts to squirm beneath me. Moving one hand down her soft tummy, my fingers dip into her belly button, running circles around the small hole. Finally, I head to the junction between her legs as she opens wider for me. I can feel wetness on her inner thighs as I kiss and nibble my way to her core. Just her smell has me ready to blow, but I need to make this good for her. My tongue lightly penetrates her as quivers run throughout her body.

Fern's hands grasp my hair, pulling me closer to the spot she wants me at the most. I start to move my tongue first, over her labia, then push into her entrance, poking in as far as I can go, then back to her engorged clit. Fern's body is out of control as she tries to move. I can tell her orgasm is approaching quickly.

I start pushing in then out of her with my tongue while my hands land on her tummy, holding her down. Increasing my speed, I hear her gasping as my tongue laps at her, grinding down on her bundle of nerves, then nibbling around it. Knowing she is ready to fly, I bite down on her clit while pumping my finger into her. Moaning, then her screams penetrate deep inside of me as my finger searches for that roughened skin deep inside of her. Once found, I begin to rub up, then down it, going round the rough patch and feel the exact minute Fern goes off the ledge, as her body clasps mine to hers refusing to release. As she floods me with her release, I feel something so deep in my heart that I lose any coherent thought.

Lifting my head I see her blushed cheeks along with some heavy panting. Moving up her body, I lie on my side, pulling her close.

"Breathe, sugar, please, just breathe."

"Oh my God, that was wonderful. Gosh, Gabriel that was... I don't even know what I want to say, honey."

Smiling up to me with so much love in her eyes, I know we have come full circle and managed to find our way back to each other, stronger than ever.

Not giving her a second to think, I reach over for a condom but before I can do anything Fern grabs it from me.

"My turn to play, honey. Lie back and enjoy."

Watching her so focused on my body, I laugh. "Sugar, what are you doing?"

"Trying to figure out where I want to go first for a taste. It has been so long, Gabriel, please be patient. I'm one hungry woman."

I feel my pulse literally takeoff at her words.

She starts kissing my neck, moving down, placing her soft mouth over my nipples, brushing them with her tongue, licking, biting, and caressing. Her small hands on my body have me going crazy and when she continues moving down my body, mouth tasting hungrily, massaging my body, hands running up and down my muscles, I feel at my wit's end.

Grabbing her under the arms, I roll over, topping her.

"Gabriel, I wasn't done."

"You are now. Fern, I can't wait, I've got to get inside you. I need to feel your warmth all around me."

Reaching for the condom yet again, I go to put it on when Fern's hands cover mine. "I want to feel just you, Gabriel, nothing else. Don't worry, no chance of pregnancy. Please, honey, I just want you, only you."

Throwing down the condom, I move back to her and very slowly I enter her. Her warmth drives me crazy and she's so fucking tight. God, I feel like I died and went to Heaven. It has been so long that my body is shaking with its need. Trying to maintain control, I grab on to Fern's shoulders looking for balance.

"Sugar, give me a minute. If we keep going, this is

not going to last long. You feel so good, baby, so damn good. I want this to be good for you."

Fern's hands are all over my body as she holds me tight inside. Feeling her trembling beneath me with her own need, I start to move slowly in and out. As we rock together, I feel the need building inside of me as the familiar feeling travels in my spine, starting to move downward as my balls tighten with need for release. God, I love this woman.

(Fern)

Watching Gabriel above me trying to maintain his control, the emotions running through me are staggering. My nipples are taut and I feel my body adjust to Gabriel's length and hardness. As he starts to pump in faster and faster, he reaches between us, running circles around my clit. I lose my breath as the release starts to build deep inside of me. My stomach tightens as the throbbing inside of me bursts. I don't want this feeling to end, but my body has already started toward an orgasm of all orgasms.

My body is glistening and humming as Gabriel changes his method by just moving his hips in circles, going deep, hitting that spot up high. As soon as his cock hits the spot, I start to feel such a wonderful feeling. I close my eyes as I start to gasp for breath, trying to let him know I am there.

"Oh my God, Gabriel, please, do not stop! Oh, God!"

The explosion takes me by surprise as I feel my body contract and hold on to his length as he continues to move in then out, faster and faster. My entire body is taut for a second and then releases to the most phenomenal feeling I have ever felt. As he continues to move inside of me, I can feel and hear the wetness from my release. I sigh in utter relief, knowing finally that my body is back to normal and that the cancer didn't win.

Gabriel starts to lose his rhythm as he chases his own release. I pull him closer, wrapping him in my arms and legs, giving him all of me. Opening myself as much as I can to give back to him all he has given me. Hearing his heavy breath on my neck as he burrows down, just as his body jerks, once, twice and then he plants himself deep in me as I feel his warmth filling me.

As we struggle to gather our breaths, he holds me close, caressing my body as we start to come back to earth.

Gabriel looks down into my eyes with such a look of love that I feel overwhelmed.

"Sugar, you take my breath away. Know how much I adore you. Fern, as I promised years ago, I will love you always."

"Gabriel, honey, that was beautiful. Now I don't

remember why I waited so long. We'll need to make up for lost time. And I'm shocked we didn't wake the kids with that racket."

Gabriel looks down at me, releasing a sweet, happy laugh.

"This is what life is all about," he says. "The closeness you share with one person who knows your heart and soul. For me it has always been and always will be you, Fern, my heart's treasure."

Holidays with the Horde

Sitting in our family room with Charlie watching football, I'm amazed at the fantastic smells coming from the kitchen. Fern, Ann, Emma, and Archie are all in there, doing whatever it is they do to create an unbelievable Thanksgiving dinner. They've been at it for hours. I was a bit shocked when I opened the door to see both Ann and Archie here so early. Ann I expected, but not Archie. She doesn't come across as the typical female because she's such a hard-ass, but she has a heart of gold. Never one to hang with the women, she's always been more comfortable hanging with us guys, drinking beer and watching sports, but since Ann's started coming around, Archie's changed... or maybe she's becoming the woman she's wanting to be.

When Ann moved into the cabin behind Wheels & Hogs with the kids, it became apparent that it was a struggle for her to take care of herself and them alone. After Lydia passed away, and I was dealing with Fern's illness, Archie and Willow gave up their apartment in town and moved into the cabin with Ann. They've created their own little family, both women seemingly love being around Ann. For Ann, it filled the void of losing her only daughter. She's taken both Archie and Willow under her wing, and Emma and Charlie adore them.

Charlie's dozing off in my lap when the doorbell rings. He's immediately up and alert, jumping off me and screaming wildly.

"Is it Cadence? Come on, let's open the door! It might be Cadence."

His excitement's contagious as we go to the door. Looking through the glass, I see Bear, Ugly, and Stash. Knowing Charlie isn't going to be happy it isn't his buddy, I lean down and whisper in his ear.

"Charlie, it's the biker dudes. Remember you wanted them to come? You invited them, so let's show them a good time. What do you say, kiddo?"

He grins wildly and swings his arms around. "Yay, the bikers are here. Let them in so we can play Legos."

Opening the door, I'm shocked to see Ugly with a bouquet of flowers, Bear holding a bottle of wine, and Stash carrying some kind of baked goods. Holy shit! They clean up good. Knowing they went Nomad from the MC club they were involved in out West before Fern's charity ride, and were actually making Tranquility their home, simply amazed me. They look the part of members of a badass club, but deep down, they're some of the nicest guys you could ever meet.

Before I can say anything, Charlie grabs Bear's free hand and pulls him in.

"Happy Thanksgiving, Bear. Let's play Legos." Laughing, Bear follows him in.

"Hey, Charlie. Let me give these to Fern first, and then we can grab the Legos. I've got something out in the bike for you too."

Charlie gets excited as the men come in, dropping their gifts into Fern's arms. She loves these guys, and it shows in the greeting they receive after she passes the gifts to Archie. They each get a hug and a kiss on the cheek. She has always been the maternal one who makes everyone welcome.

I see the look Ugly has on his face when he realizes Archie's here. When he turns away from her, I see it written all over his face—he wants Archie. I'll have to speak to Fern about this, 'cause I'm not sure they would be a good fit for each other, and Fern will make sure no one ends up hurt.

The doorbell rings again, and Charlie comes running to greet the newcomers. Des and Dee Dee, along with her kids, Jagger and Daisy, stand in the front. The Powers family, Cadence, Trinity, along with baby Hope is standing right behind them. I open the door wide, letting everyone in, and notice how unhappy Daisy seems.

As everyone greets each other, Des and Cadence drop off their handfuls of food before making their way back outside to get whatever else is left in their cars. Once they return, I step back to take in the people Fern and I consider family, but a familiar face is missing. I look around and find Daisy sitting in the far corner of the family room on the floor, and for the first time, I notice how gaunt she looks. She looks like she's lost quite a bit of weight since I saw her last, and it's weight she couldn't't afford to lose. Her eyes have black circles under them, but what stands out the most is that she's alienating herself from her family. Something serious is going on with her, so I make a mental note to have a word with Des…

Grab your copy and have some fun during the Holidays with the Horde (Book 4).

CANCER RESOURCES

I hope you enjoyed Gabriel & Fern's story. The subject matter of cancer has touched each and every one of us at some time in our lives. I dedicate this book to everyone who has been touched by cancer in one way or another. Never give up the fight.

Resources:
   http://www.cancer.org/
   http://www.canceradvocacy.org/resources/
   http://www.acor.org/

ABOUT THE AUTHOR

USA Today Bestselling author D. M. Earl spins stories about real life situations with characters that are authentic, genuine and sincere. Each story allows the characters to come to life with each turn of the page while they try to find their HEA through much drama and angst.

When not writing, DM loves to read some of her favorite authors books. Also she loves to spend quality time with her hubby & family along with her 7 fur babies. When weather permits she likes to ride her Harley.

Contact D.M at DM@DMEARL.COM
Website: http://www.dmearl.com/

- facebook.com/DMEarlAuthorIndie
- twitter.com/dmearl
- instagram.com/dmearl14
- amazon.com/D-M-Earl/e/B00M2HB12U
- bookbub.com/authors/d-m-earl
- goodreads.com/dmearl
- pinterest.com/dauthor

ALSO BY D.M. EARL

DEVIL'S HANDMAIDENS MC: TIMBER-GHOST, MONTANA CHAPTER

Tink (Book #1)

GRIMM WOLVES MC SERIES

Behemoth (Book 1)

Bottom of the Chains-Prospect (Book 2)

Santa...Nope The Grimm Wolves (Book 3)

Keeping Secrets-Prospect (Book 4)

A Tormented Man's Soul: Part One (Book 5)

Triad Resumption: Part Two (Book 6)

WHEELS & HOGS SERIES

Connelly's Horde (Book 1)

Cadence Reflection (Book 2)

Gabriel's Treasure (Book 3)

Holidays with the Horde (Book 4)

My Sugar (Book 5)

Daisy's Darkness (Book 6)

THE JOURNALS TRILOGY

Anguish (Book 1)

Vengeance (Book 2)

Awakening (Book 3)

STAND ALONE TITLES

Survivor: A Salvation Society Novel

Printed in Great Britain
by Amazon